MW00876761

Teenage Treasure Hunter

DANIEL KENNEY

Trendwood Press

Copyright © 2015 Daniel Kenney
All rights reserved.
Published by Trendwood Press

No part of this publication may be reproduced or transmitted in any form or by any means, electronic or mechanical, including photography, recording, or any information storage and retrieval system without the prior written consent from the publisher and author, except in the instance of quotes for reviews. No part of this book may be uploaded without the permission of the publisher and author, nor be otherwise circulated in any form of binding or cover other than that in which it is originally published.

This is a work of fiction and any resemblance to persons, living or dead, or places, actual events or locales is purely coincidental. The characters and names are products of the authors imagination and used fictitiously.

The publisher and author acknowledge the trademark status and trademark ownership of all trademarks, service marks and word marks mentioned in this book.

To my father, who taught me to love history

CHAPTER ONE

THE DOLLS

Curial ran to the top of the steps and read the pink Post-it note again.

I gave this to you because I knew you could do it.
Trust me,
Mom

After three days of staring at the note, Curial still had no idea what it meant. *Gave me what? Do what?* He shook his head and entered the museum.

A security guard unfolded the *New York Times* and flashed an easy smile.

"Do you know where Claude is?" Curial asked, while tapping his foot against the polished marble.

"Just passed by here a couple minutes ago. You want me to call him up?"

Curial shook his head. "Don't worry about it. He can't

be too far."

The guard shrugged while Curial gripped the note tightly and practically sprinted down the corridor. He stopped when something caught his eye to his left. Something important. Finding Claude could wait a minute.

He turned and made his way toward a rectangular portrait hanging in the corner. Curial stopped, drew his breath and sat down on a shiny wooden bench. Then he loosened the grip on the note and looked up at the painting. At the woman in the painting. She wore a full-length grey dress, appeared to be in her early thirties, and stood between an armed soldier and a boy. Her lips curled into a subtle smile.

Curial's mom had loved this painting. She loved how the anonymous Dutch painter alternated his use of heavy and light brush strokes to add layers of interest to the piece. She loved how the woman and the boy were people of color like themselves. But mostly, his mom loved how the woman protected the little boy—and how, in the midst of everything looking so dark and hopeless, she still found a reason to smile.

This woman *knew* something.

Curial turned away from the picture when he saw a familiar man approaching: MAC Art Director Claude Von Kerstens. Claude was the only employee of the

Wall Street Journal. Said he needed his son to be on top of the latest news, especially anything that might impact banking or the economy.

After breakfast, Curial rode the back elevator down to the gymnasium. Hank was already bouncing around the ring, gloves and headgear on, ready to spar.

"Come, Master Diggs. I watched a particularly thrilling episode of *Survivor* last night and feel inspired to kick your skinny can all over the ring today."

Curial put on his headgear and gloves, then climbed into the ring. "You'll have to catch me first, Limpy."

Hank raised an eyebrow. "Having one leg shorter than the other is nothing to laugh at. I'll have you know that two out of every ten people suffer from short-leggedness, and these brave souls walk around every day without anybody being any the wiser."

"Yeah, until they slip into the ring with Kid Dynamo and his cougar-like reflexes." Curial slipped his mouth guard in. "You ready?"

Hank lifted one glove into the air. "Ding, ding."

Curial faked left, then faked right. Hank threw exactly one punch, a jab that hit Curial in the forehead. Curial fell flat on his butt.

The proper English butler stood over his boss.

Curial spit out his mouth guard. "Go ahead, you know you want to."

"Pardon me, Master Diggs, but an English butler does not gloat."

Curial stumbled to his feet. "Just one more thing Americans are better at than the English?"

Hank shook his head. "It does, however, feel quite good to put you in your proper place."

After sparring for twenty minutes, Hank took Curial to the pull-up bar. Four impressive sets later, Curial fell to the mat, his arms and back exhausted. When he looked up, he was staring at the climbing wall, the one his mom had had custom-built for them.

Hank cleared his throat. "You know, Master Diggs, as much as it pains me to say it, you've developed an impressive amount of strength on the pull-up bar; I'm sure with me manning the ropes, that wall would be a cinch for you."

Curial's heart started beating again and his arms went clammy. He backed up.

"I—I can't."

Hank raised a finger and Curial cut him off with a wave of his hand.

"I said I can't."

*_*_*

Curial rode the back elevator to the fourth floor, where the doors opened onto a medium-sized foyer. Straight in front of him was the set of stairs leading down to the third floor; to his left was a single oak door with a circular stained-glass window. It led into the chapel that his grandfather had built.

Curial's grandmother had been fond of saying that the secret to success is that there *is* no secret: just hard work and faith in God. Curial spent a great deal of time testing his own faith in God during the final weeks of his mom's life. For hours and hours he'd prayed for her in his grandfather's chapel. Sometimes he wondered if maybe he hadn't prayed hard enough, or if his faith hadn't been strong enough or, maybe, just maybe, God simply hadn't heard his prayers.

To Curial's right were two large hand-carved oak doors. He grabbed their brushed copper handles and pulled them open, revealing his favorite part of the Diggs Mansion: the library.

Correction: *his* library.

Curial's grandfather designed the original library, and it still retained its old charm. The main floor was covered in wide-plank quarter-sawn oak which, although eighty years old, looked almost new. Huge dark walnut bookshelves formed a giant U around a large rectangular table—said to have been made from the wood of an old fishing boat from the early 1900s. A beautiful spiral staircase led to the second floor. All in all, it was a fitting showcase for the hundreds and hundreds of leather-bound books the library held.

Curial climbed the stairs—he could handle stairs—to the second floor, which looked much like the first, minus the rectangular table. The walnut bookcases wrapped around the balcony in another U, and Curial walked along the railing until he reached the middle of that U. There he spotted the special copy of *Swiss Family Robinson*. The book was a recent addition to the library: one of a few high-tech modifications that Curial's mom had allowed him to make in order to bring the old library into the new millennium.

Curial gripped the book, one of his favorites as a child, and pulled it straight out. When he did, he heard the sound of metal clicking against metal, followed by a whoosh, and a doorway opened up in the middle of the bookcase. He walked through to a large, well-lit interior room, with two computers, two wall monitors, and a large, clear glass desk in the center. He pushed a button on the glass table and the monitors and computers sprang to life.

After a moment of electronic humming, a voice crackled from a nearby speaker.

"Good morning, Curial."

Curial set the Post-it note on the glass table and stared at it for a few minutes, trying again to make sense of it.

When nothing magical happened, he crumpled up the note and tossed it into the corner. *Time to move on.*

Curial opened up a special search window. He always routed his searches through IP addresses in other countries, so they'd be more difficult to trace back to him. If his dad ever learned he was spending most of his time looking for treasure in Peru instead of learning how to read financial statements, Curial would be on the next train to Haverfield.

At some point Mabel brought him lunch, and by midafternoon Curial was starting to get sleepy, so he turned up the music to power through the sugar crash. He was singing loudly to "Paint It Black" by the Rolling Stones when, out of his peripheral vision, he noticed a green light blinking. It took him a moment to realize what it meant. An intruder. Crap. The music had been too loud and he hadn't heard the buzzer.

He spun around and almost jumped out of his skin.

Getty, his father's assistant, stood five feet away from him, arms folded, shaking his head back and forth; the scowl was chiseled deep as ever into his face.

Curial tried to control his breathing, his heart feeling like it might jump out of his chest. He turned the music down and Getty shook his head.

"So this is what you do all day? Hide away in your secret bat cave, listening to rock and roll while playing with the fanciest computers money can buy?" Getty rolled his eyes as he bent down to look at the computer screen. Curial jumped in front of him.

"What do you want, Getty?"

Getty straightened up and glared. "What do I want? I'd give anything to have what you have. But I promise you, instead of wasting it looking at God-only-knows-what in Peru, I would work hard to *earn* the job that will one day be handed to you on a silver platter."

"You don't know anything about me."

Getty did what he did best: he rolled his eyes. "Whatever."

Curial locked eyes with Getty. He wanted to demonstrate the new left-right combination Hank had taught him in the ring. He wanted to drag him down the spiral staircase by the collar of his perfectly tailored suit.

"Why exactly are you here?" Curial asked.

Getty stood unfazed, unmoving for twenty seconds, then finally grabbed a green folder out of his brown leather satchel.

"To give you this. After you left yesterday, your father remembered one more place I should look. Turns out your mother *did* leave you something."

She did?

Curial stared at the folder for a moment, not fully understanding, then finally grabbed it and looked up at his dad's assistant. "Thanks."

Getty rolled his eyes once more and took another look around the corners of the secret room. "Some of us have *real* work to do." He spun and walked down the length of the balcony, descended the spiral staircase, and left the library.

Curial stared at the front doors of the library for a full minute after Getty left, then realized his body was so tense he was practically crushing the folder in his hands. A green folder with a little bump on the bottom. He turned it over. The flaps of the folder were attached together with a blood red seal made out of wax. It had two initials impressed into it: *C.D.*

Caroline Diggs.

Curial Diggs.

Curial's heart raced. He ran back into his computer room, laid the folder on his glass desk, and ripped open the seal.

Inside was a handwritten note, in his mother's handwriting:

Dear Curial,

The first dream of my life was to have a son, and I couldn't be more proud of you and the young man you've become.

The second dream of my life was to one day find

the treasure that bewitched me in my youth. Over my life, I've accumulated a special folder with everything I know about the Romanov Dolls and their disappearance.

Curial, I want you to continue where I left off.

I want you to find the treasure—but only when you're ready. And you will know you're ready when you can find that special folder. Consider it a small treasure hunt to see if you've got what it takes for the grander adventure.

Good luck, my wonderful boy. As the only son of your father, much is expected of you. But you are also my son. And I always hope you can follow your heart.

Love,

Mom

P.S. Turn the sheet over for your clue.

CHAPTER FOUR

THE CLUE

Curial read the clue for the third time.

HA J E F 18 19 4 12 15

Gibberish. Nonsense. Curial drummed his fingers against the glass table. He looked at the clue again. Tilted his head. He thought of what the letters and numbers might represent, but the only thing that made any sense was a license plate. Could that possibly be it? Maybe his mom hid something in one of the many cars in the Diggs family automobile fleet. He took out his cell and dialed his driver.

"Mike, do we have any cars with the following license plate number?" He spoke slowly as he read off the sequence of letters and numbers.

Mike sounded like he was gurgling water. "That's too long for a license plate."

"But the first part of it, with the letters, that could be a license plate. Does it ring a bell?"

"Curial, your family has over forty cars that I maintain and drive—across three different residences in the state of New York alone. I don't have all the plates memorized."

"Yeah, of course."

"But I do have them all listed in my records. Give me a second."

Curial heard the echoes of Mike's footfalls as he walked across the concrete of the family's parking garage.

"Okay," Mike said, "running through the list right now. Hmmmm. Nope. Got nothing for H A J E F."

"Can you think of any other cars or license plates that would mean something to my mom?"

"Nah. Curial, your mom wasn't much of a car lady. What's this about anyway?"

"Never mind, dead end."

Curial puzzled over the letters that evening, ran them through his computer for some kind of recognition, and found nothing promising. By the looks of it, the letters were random. Which made him think the letters might stand for something *else*—like an acronym. So he tried to think of words that started with these letters. Words that might mean something to his mom. Like a famous quote, something like that. He brainstormed the rest of the night, trying different combinations, but ultimately he came up with nothing.

The next morning, while Curial ate some of Mabel's

crunchy French toast, he ignored the *Wall Street Journal* in favor of continuing to play with the letters and numbers from his mom's clue.

"Good morning, Master Diggs," Hank said from behind him. "Should I be arranging an ambulance for you after this morning's workout?"

"Ah, yeah, sure thing," Curial said, not taking his eyes from the clue for even a moment.

"Master Diggs, are you feeling quite well? I don't detect even a hint of your usual insufferable self this morning."

Curial looked up.

"Oh, hi, Hank. Were you talking to me?"

"You appear preoccupied, sir." Hank bent down over Curial's shoulder. "What is it that you're working out?"

Curial shook his head. "Not sure. It's something Mom left me. She said it was a clue of some sort, but I can't wrap my brain around it."

"And she left it for you?"

"Yep."

"So she must have made it something you *can* figure out."

Curial nodded. "But so far, no luck. Look here, do these letters ring a bell to you?" Curial spread the napkin out so Hank could see.

Hank bent low again and squinted, then shook his

head. "No, nothing at all, sir. They seem, well, random. There doesn't appear to be any order at all."

"Right," said Curial. "And why would my mom give me a clue with letters and numbers that have no order?"

Hank smiled. "I don't believe she would, sir. In the army, we had a word for letters and numbers that appeared to have no order."

"Yeah, what's that?" Curial said, spinning a pencil between his fingers.

"A code."

Curial shrugged. "Clue, code, same difference."

Hank shook his head. "To the riffraff still inhabiting the American colonies maybe, but as for those speaking the King's English, not really."

Curial sat up a little straighter. "I'm offended and curious all at the same time."

"A *clue* functions more like a symbol," Hank explained. "A clue reminds you of something else. The whole point of a *code* is for it to not remind you of anything. The army transmits messages in codes so enemies won't figure them out."

Curial tapped his pencil against his napkin.

"So, how to decipher this code?"

"Codes have keys, Master Diggs. If this is a code, then there's some key that opens it up."

Curial wrinkled his forehead. "Like what?"

"I don't have the faintest idea, Master Diggs. You're the generation that tumbles, tweets, and faceplants."

"You mean Facebooks?"

"My point exactly. You're smart enough to figure it out."

"Speaking on behalf of the American riffraff, could you please give me a hint?"

Hank rolled his eyes. "It could be anything. The receiver of the code might have a piece of paper with a key that says the letter H stands for, I don't know, an airplane. Or that each number stands for a different letter in the alphabet. Or each letter stands—"

"Wait, go back. What was the second thing you said?"

"Each number stands for a letter?"

Curial slapped the table. "I'm an idiot."

"I think that's been well established, sir." Hank bowed slightly, then left the kitchen via the swinging door.

When Curial was seven, his mom took him to Coney Island on a hot July day. She told him that if they became separated for any reason, he should just yell "Mom" as loud as he could and she would find him.

He remembered how he was too embarrassed and refused to do it. "No boy my age calls for their mom in public," he told her.

She thought about it a minute, counted something on her fingers, then wrote down the letters of the alphabet on her hand. Underneath the letter A, she wrote a zero, under the letter B she wrote a one, and so on until she had finished assigning each letter of the alphabet its own number. When she finished, she circled the M and the number below it:12. Then she circled the O and the number below it: 14.

"So, Curial," she asked, "how would you spell Mom using numbers?"

He puzzled over it for a bit, then smiled as he tapped on the palm of her hand. "Twelve, fourteen, twelve?"

She nodded. "So next time you're embarrassed about saying 'Mom,' just use this special code instead."

He remembered how strange that sounded. "You want me to call you twelve-fourteen-twelve?"

"Too weird?" she asked.

He nodded and thought about it until he came up with a solution.

"Mom, if I add up all three numbers they equal thirty-eight. Can I just call you thirty-eight instead?"

Occasionally, over the years since, he had still called his mom thirty-eight from time to time, but he had mostly forgotten about how the nickname started.

Until just now.

Curial grabbed a napkin and wrote down the letters A through K, and then put a 0 under the A, a 1 under the B, and so on, just like his mom had done.

Then he matched them up. Now, instead of H A J E F, he had 7 0 9 4 5.

He had assumed that unlocking a code would reveal something that made sense. But these numbers didn't.

So he did the same thing with the numbers. 18 corresponded with S in the alphabet. 19 corresponded with T, 4 corresponded with E and so forth, until at the end he wrote out everything that he had.

7 0 9 4 5 S T E M

He grouped the numbers and the letters separately.

70945 STEM

He said it to himself once, twice, three times before it suddenly clicked. His mom's code had revealed *another* code. Except that, normally, there was a period between the 9 and the 4 in this particular code: *709.45*.

709.45 STEM was an example of a popular kind of code used to organize books in libraries all over the world: the Dewey Decimal System. And this particular Dewey Decimal number referenced a book from the Arts section of the library. Specifically, Renaissance Art.

Of all the books on art his mom had ever shown him, Curial wondered which book his mom wanted him to find. There was one way to find out.

He took out his phone and sent Mike Douglas a text.

"Be ready in ten. We've got a trip to make."

CHAPTER FIVE

MAURICE

Mike dropped Curial off at Fifth Avenue and 42nd Street in front of the Stephen A. Schwarzman Building. It served as the main branch of the New York City Library and, to Curial's mother, was one of the most beautiful buildings in all of New York. Built at the turn of the twentieth century, the Schwarzman Building had once been the world's largest marble building and included an enormous and majestic reading room that was among Curial's most favorite spots.

He went to the Arts section of the library, found the spot for the 709's, and located 709.45 STEM on the fourth shelf up. When he pulled the book out, he remembered it at once. Richard Stemp's *The Secret Language of the Renaissance*.

A couple of years earlier, his mother had let him take a break from his Pre-Algebra lessons and had taken him to the library instead. She'd grabbed this book off the shelf and taken it to the reading room, where she showed Curial pictures of famous paintings, sculptures, and churches. Then she came to a particular page and, like she so often did, asked Curial what he saw.

He couldn't now remember the page, but he would never forget the piece of art. So he found it in the index, then turned to the page: page 168. And there it was, just as he remembered it from that day.

"Well if it isn't the rich kid who likes to give me his money?"

Curial spun around. Unbelievable. It was that punk skateboarding kid.

"You?" Curial said. "You just about killed me yesterday."

The kid smirked. "I think if you check the New York City statutes, skateboarders have the right of way on sidewalks."

"That's the dumbest thing I've ever heard," said Curial.

Now, the kid shrugged. "Whatever, so you're clumsy, how is that my problem?"

"And a few weeks ago, you stole a hundred bucks from me."

"I believe I won it from you and, forgive me your majesty, but have you looked at your house lately. I think you can afford a hundred bucks." He leaned in. "So what do you got there?"

"Nothing you would understand," said Curial.

"Ahh, because I'm just a dumb street kid, eh?"

"I didn't say you were dumb. Just, um..."

The kid leaned in closer.

"Looks like a vestibule to me."

Curial was surprised. "How on earth could you possibly know that?"

The kid pointed. "Because of the word *vestibule* right below the picture."

Curial felt like a moron. "Yeah, well, a vestibule is like an entrance."

"I gathered that, Einstein." The kid pointed again. "Because right here it says 'a vestibule is like an entrance.'"

"Why are *you* here?" asked Curial.

The kid looked around. "Me? Well, first of all, I've got a name other than *you*. It's Maurice. Second, I'm here because," he lowered his voice to a whisper, "don't tell anybody, but it's a library, and I like to read."

"*You*," said Curial. "You like to read?"

"Do you have to practice to be that condescending or does it come natural when you have a chauffeur drive you everywhere? I said the name was Maurice, practice saying it with me, MAURICE."

Curial tensed up. "You are such a—"

"Curious kid named Maurice who wants to know more

about this vestibule." The kid grinned. "Why are you looking at it?"

"Does Maurice really want to know?"

"Yeah sure."

Curial hesitated. He really should just tell this Maurice to get lost. That's what his father would do. But it wasn't what his mother would do. Curial took a breath. "Fine, this is the vestibule of the Laurentian Library, in Florence, Italy. It was designed by the greatest of all Renaissance artists—and one of the greatest artistic geniuses in all of human history. Bet you can't guess who."

Maurice held up a finger. "My money's on one of the Teenage Mutant Ninja Turtles."

"It was Michelangelo," said Curial.

"That's the really immature one who uses nunchuks and likes pizza, right?"

Curial shook his head. "You're an idiot. We're talking about the greatest artist in history, not a turtle. From the *Pieta*, his sculpture depicting Mary holding her son Jesus after his death, to the magnificent dome adorning St. Peter's Basilica; from the beautiful frescoes painted onto the ceiling of the Sistine Chapel, to the absolute perfection of the *David*. Michelangelo did all of it." Curial could see Maurice's eyes start to glaze over.

"Why am I trying to explain this to you? I'm sure you have someone to run over, rob, or generally annoy as much as humanly possible."

The kid shook his head. "Nah, I'm pretty content to just annoy you right now. So why's a rich kid all alone in the library staring at pictures of a vestibule? Seems kinda weird."

"You wouldn't understand," said Curial.

"Bet I would."

"Promise to leave me alone if I tell you?"

"Even better," Maurice pulled a watch out of his pocket. "I promise to give you this back."

"That's my watch!"

"And that's why I'm offering it back to you," said Maurice. "Wouldn't make much sense to offer you someone else's watch, now would it?"

"You stole my watch! You little—" Curial snatched it out of Maurice's hand. "Go away!"

Maurice smirked. "Dude, kinda grumpy considering I just found your watch."

"Yeah," said Curial, "you found it on *my* wrist."

Maurice held up his finger. "A minor technicality. Now I believe we had an arrangement, so what's the deal with the vestibule?"

Curial shook his head and tapped his foot. "I explain it to you and you promise to leave me alone?"

"Promise."

"Fine," said Curial. "My mom was really into art, okay?

She knew I was a big fan of Michelangelo—"

"Not the wise cracking, pizza loving, turtle in a half shell right?"

Curial continued, "—and anyways, she wanted to show me this picture of the Laurentian Library vestibule. The vestibule was the entrance room that somebody would pass through before, in this case, walking into the main reading room of the library."

Curial hesitated, remembering the first time he saw the vestibule, with its overly wide marble staircase and hand-carved stone treatments.

"Well, Curial? What do you think?" his mom had finally asked him.

He'd remembered feeling confusion. Here was Michelangelo, maybe the greatest artist in history, and yet, something about this vestibule just wasn't right.

"It's a beautiful marble staircase in a pretty room," he had said, a little cautiously.

His mother had given him that quizzical look where her eyebrows would pinch together and her nose would scrunch up. She tapped on the picture. "Okay. I'll give you that. But here's why I'm showing you this picture, Curial. With art, sometimes the thing is just beautiful. It just is what it is. And sometimes, well, sometimes there's more to it, and you have to read between the lines."

"Read between the lines?"

She nodded and smiled. He missed her smile.

A snap in front of his face jolted him back.

"Earth to rich kid, earth to rich kid," said Maurice.

"What?" Curial said.

"You spaced out there dude. You were saying something and then you went to lala land."

"Yeah," Curial returned to the book. "So look at this picture, think about all the amazing things you've ever seen Michelangelo the artist do."

Maurice leaned over, squinting.

"Okay," said Curial, "now tell me what you think of this vestibule."

Maurice shrugged. "Honestly?"

Curial nodded.

"It's not very good."

"Be specific," Curial said. "In what way is it not very good?"

Curial's own thoughts immediately went to the utter perfection of the dome at St. Peter's, or the beautiful simplicity of the *David*.

"Well," Maurice said, outlining the vestibule with his finger, "this room, this vestibule, it's not that big—but the staircase takes up the entire room. The whole thing appears crowded and stuffy."

Curial smiled. "Good. Anything else?"

"Well, look at those stone brackets," Maurice said,

pointing to some decorative stone carvings jutting out of the side walls. "You'd think they have some kind of purpose, like to support something above them. But here, they look sort of splattered onto the wall for decoration. Like they *have* no purpose."

"Excellent. And what feelings does this piece give you?"

Maurice shrugged. "Feelings? Dude, I thought we were talking about this picture."

"Fine, like when you see the picture does it seem balanced and harmonious?"

"Uh, negatory, Doctor Vocabulary. The whole thing seems, I don't know, scrunched."

Curial was almost impressed. For a pick-pocket-idiot-skate boarder, Maurice was quick. "Well, I'm not sure you will be a first-class art critic one day, but that was actually pretty good. But now is the time for the one-million-dollar question. Why? Why would Michelangelo, possibly the most brilliant artist in history, have built something so scrunched? Do you think he was just having a bad day?"

Maurice tapped his finger against his forehead. "So you're saying he did it on purpose?"

"Yep. My mom taught me that sometimes the thing is the thing itself, and sometimes you have to read between the lines."

"I don't know what you mean by that."

Curial pointed to a paragraph of text next to the picture. "The author explains how with *this* piece of art," Curial began reading from the book, '*Michelangelo was trying to get people to escape the darkness and confusion of their own ignorance by climbing physically, and then intellectually, toward the source of inspiration. The source of inspiration, in the case of the Laurentian Library, was of course its grand reading room, where people could access books. And the reading room itself, in sharp contrast to the vestibule, was simple, balanced, orderly, and beautiful.*'".

"Whoa," said Maurice, "I didn't understand any of that and I'm afraid if you keep talking, I'll fall asleep."

"You're the one who asked."

"Yeah, well, I'm a little sorry I did." Maurice fished something out of his back pocket. It was a wallet.

"You *also* took my wallet?" said Curial.

Maurice made a face. "Yeah, you'd think a rich kid like yourself would be more careful with his stuff."

"No, what I should do is call the cops."

"And I believe that's my cue to leave. Until the next time I can win a hundred bucks from you or get a boring art lecture." Maurice smiled as he tilted his head, then he spun around and walked away and Curial was certain he had just met the most irritating person in history. He checked his pockets to make sure nothing else was missing, then he returned to the picture of the vestibule.

As he did, he could hear, really *hear* his mom's voice: *Read between the lines, Curial.* Somewhere in this picture was his mom's next message.

He looked, stared, rotated the painting, tried to remember anything else she might have told him. Nothing. He blew out a sharp breath. What was he missing? What would his mom expect him to do? He stood the book up, leaning it against some other books, took two steps back, and studied the painting again. Seeing nothing in particular, he moved slowly forward—and something small caught his eye. But not from the painting. From the page *opposite* the painting, where there was printed text describing the piece of art.

Something was out of place.

Curial moved his face closer to the page. There, between the first and second line, was a tiny handwritten number: the number '4'. And then Curial spotted another, between the second and third lines of text: a '0'.

Could his mother want him to literally *read between the lines?*

Curial scanned down the page: sure enough, between each line of text and the next was another number. He pulled out a scratch pad and furiously wrote them down in order. Along the way was a period, then some more numbers, a comma, a dash, then more numbers. Finally, when he reached the bottom of the page, he looked at what he'd written down.

40.8009833, -73.9587055

And this time, Curial recognized the numbers at once.

CHAPTER SIX

COMING TOGETHER

Curial had worked enough with mapping programs to recognize Global Positioning Satellite coordinates. He took out his phone and punched the GPS coordinates into Google Maps; a red dot popped up at the northwest corner of Central Park in Harlem. A coffee shop on the other side of Frederick Douglass Circle.

Café Amrita.

That didn't necessarily click, but the GPS coordinates were unmistakable. His mom wanted him at, or very near, that coffee shop. As he left the library, he found Mike eating a hot dog outside.

"Is that one of those vegetarian hot dogs I've been hearing so much about?" Curial asked, shaking his head.

Mike wiped mustard off the edges of his mouth. "I just had to try it, to see if in fact this was the finest hot dog in

New York." He pointed to the sign on the front of a nearby vendor stand: *Police Dogs, New York's Finest.* "I'm sorry to say that I've been bamboozled. There are at least two hot dog stands better in Manhattan alone. And Queens? Don't even get me started."

"Well, we're heading to the northwest corner of Central Park. Think they'll be any hot dogs for you to judge there?"

Mike hustled around the car and opened up the driver's side door. "Curial, you know me. I won't like it, but my stomach's ready for duty anytime."

Fifteen minutes later, Mike was off in search of another hot dog stand at the end of the park while Curial walked to a spot on the sidewalk just in front of Café Amrita. Three sets of white double doors were open, and the rich smell of ground coffee drifted outside.

Curial studied the simple sign written on the awning above the doors. He looked at the sidewalk. At the shops next to the Café. Mom had left a clue for him at this place, he was sure of it. He just didn't know where to look.

He went inside and ordered a white chocolate mocha, then sat down at a small brown table against the wall and relaxed while he sipped his coffee. Why did his mother want him at this coffee shop? What was so special about Café Amrita? He had spent a lot of time with his mother, but she'd never taken him here. Never even mentioned it.

He looked at the other customers and the people that worked here. Did they know his mom? Maybe he could show them her picture? He made a few people uncomfortable with his staring before, finally, about to give up on the coffee shop, he walked to the back in order to use the restroom. On the way he passed a community bulletin board, and something caught his eye.

A sign above the community bulletin board said *Between The Lines.*

Curial spun around and found the nearest barista.

"Excuse me," Curial asked, his heart beating a little faster. "Why does it say *Between The Lines* above your bulletin board?"

The woman was grinding beans into a cup. She shrugged. "No idea. That's just what our bulletin board has always been called." She rolled her eyes. "Our manager thinks it's cute. He tells people to go read *between the lines* for what's going on in the neighborhood."

Curial thanked her, then went back to the board. There was a mess of things pinned and taped to the board. Business cards for cleaning services; a photo of a lost poodle; a few concert flyers; a bicycle repair shop advertising their services; three flyers from people looking for a roommate. Nothing that looked like something his mom would have wanted him to see.

But Curial's mom had been gone for more than six months. Anything she had pinned would probably be gone by now. *Which means she wouldn't have pinned it.*

Curial realized his mom wouldn't have given him a clue so temporary. So he lifted up the flyers, peeking at the board underneath, until, in the middle of the board, under a flyer for home painting, he found it. There, in black permanent marker, was the elegant handwriting of his mother. He removed the painting flyer and pinned it on a different part of the board, then studied the words in front of him.

Among the ranks and files of the park
Your quest begins in the dark
The gospel writer you will find
And you'll be checked by the blind

A riddle. His mom loved riddles. Dad loved numbers and financial statements and discussions of the Federal Reserve; he never saw the point in doing the *New York Times* crossword or the books of riddles mom would do late at night in bed. But Mom loved them.

Curial's mom had taught him to approach riddles kind of like art. Ask yourself what comes to your mind first. Your gut reaction. Then hold it off to the side. You might use it—you might not. Then go over the riddles several times as a whole. Then isolate the chunks.

His first impression was that the rank and file of the park could either be the normal people who walk through the park every day, or maybe the bums that live in the park. That the dark part of the park would be hidden in the trees somewhere. That the gospel writer must refer to something related to the Bible, and that whatever he did would have something to do with being able to do it with his eyes closed.

But those gut reactions didn't make any cohesive sense. So Curial went slower and deeper.

He went back to the first line:

Among the ranks and files of the park

Okay, that was strange. Normally you think of the phrase "rank and file"—which, Curial knew, referred to the common people. But "ranks and files" was a different phrase—and so it must be different *on purpose*. In riddles, the subtle differences mattered. Something about this phrase gnawed at his brain, but he couldn't quite make sense of it. So he moved on:

Your quest begins in the dark

Now this could mean a couple of things. Either it referred to the fact that he was "in the dark" and didn't know much about the Romanov Dolls, or it meant he was supposed to start the quest under the trees or in a cave. He puzzled over that for a few minutes, then continued on to the next line:

The gospel writer you will find

The more he thought about this line, the less it seemed like the Bible itself, and more like a clue to a name. Maybe Matthew, Mark, Luke, or John. But why? Was there something inside the park that was named for one of the gospel writers? He knew the park pretty well, but nothing about the gospel writers' names rang any bells.

Finally, Curial examined the last line:

And you'll be checked by the blind

He shook his head. This one made no sense at all. What could it possibly mean to be checked by the blind?

Checked, checked, checked. The only way that "checked" might make sense was in hockey, and he couldn't think of what kind of hockey reference his mom would use. She hated hockey, and football, and any of the normal sports. The only sport she truly loved was...

Chess.

Checked.

That was it. *That's* the other way in which he knew the word "checked." As in "checkmate."

And then something else made sense, like pieces of a puzzle falling into place. If this had something to do with chess, then he understood the reference to ranks and files. Ranks and files referred to the rows and columns of a chessboard.

Somehow, this clue was supposed to lead him to the chessboards that were often set up inside the park. The park he was staring at through the window of the coffee shop.

Central Park.

Curial left the coffee shop, crossed Frederick Douglass Circle, and found Mike a hundred yards away, testing a chili cheese dog.

Mike gave Curial a thumbs-up. "This dog gets the Mike Douglas Seal of Approval."

"Mike, are there any chess players down on this end of the park?"

A bit of chili spilled down Mike's chin. He nodded toward the park as he wiped it up with the side of his hand.

"There's a group of serious players who meet not too far from here. By the way, on a scale of one jelly donut to ten jelly donuts I give this hotdog a—

But Curial never heard him; he was already gone,

jogging into the park. Within minutes he saw a group of men off to his left, gathered around a few small round metal tables, playing chess.

For some reason he couldn't begin to understand, his mom was directing him to these chess tables. He considered the line about his quest beginning in the dark. Even though trees surrounded the tables, plenty of sunlight came through—this spot wasn't really in the dark. He considered the next line, about the gospel writers. He decided to look for any evidence of something, anything, named after Matthew, Mark, Luke, or John. He nodded at a man who was contemplating his next chess move, and walked over to examine a plaque at the base of a tree.

In memory of Megan Dolan, the plaque said.

That's when something in the hum of the chess conversation caught his ear. A name.

Mark.

Curial turned toward where he thought the conversation was coming from. A skinny black man, wearing sweats and a hoodie, was playing against a wide-shouldered, barrel-chested white man in a big orange Hawaiian shirt.

Curial listened in on their conversation, and heard the skinny black guy call the big white guy "Mark" again. He wandered closer, and was surprised when the white man called the black man "Luke."

Well, there's two of the gospel writers. But maybe that was just a coincidence.

The skinny guy saw Curial watching them and gave him a friendly nod. "You play?"

"A little," Curial replied, embarrassed to have been caught snooping.

"Good, then you've got something in common with Mark here. He plays a very *little* brand of chess." Luke laughed and slapped his knee.

Mark grunted and leaned in closer to the chessboard. "Shut up, before I beat you over the head with my king."

Mark grabbed his pawn and started to move it, but then his eyes lifted up to Luke, who was shaking his head slowly back and forth. Mark put the pawn back, grabbed his knight instead, and moved quickly. Luke laughed again.

"Excuse me, guys," Curial interrupted before Luke started his own move. "You mind if I ask you a question? Did I hear you right, Luke and Mark?"

Luke grabbed his queen and nodded. "Yep, just like the gospel boys."

This had to be it. "You wouldn't by chance know a woman named Caroline Diggs?"

They looked at each other and frowned.

Mark scratched his chin while examining the

chessboard again. "Does she play chess down here?"

"Honestly," Curial said, a bit disappointed, "I'm not sure. Just thought someone around here might know her."

Luke shrugged.

"You know kid, there's a guy that's been around here a lot longer than us. Knows everyone."

"Who?"

Luke pointed a long gangly finger. "That guy over by the tree, with his back turned."

"Thanks. What's his name?"

The skinny guy smiled. "Matthew, of course."

Curial's heart quickened as he walked toward the man. Matthew was black, graying at the temples, and Curial could hear his laugh from about thirty feet away. Then Curial saw something and stopped.

Leaning against the tree next to the man was a long, skinny white stick. The kind of stick used only by certain people.

People who are blind.

And then it all came together.

And you'll be checked by the blind

CHAPTER SEVEN

GETTY

Curial's mother wanted him to play this blind man Matthew in a game of chess. He was certain of it.

As Curial watched, Matthew yelled out "checkmate!" and the younger man he was playing shook his head, almost in disbelief. The old man extended his hand, long fingers grown slightly crooked from an even longer life, and the young man took it and thanked him. Then the young man grabbed his backpack, jumped on his bike, and rode off.

Matthew started to rearrange the pieces like he'd probably done thousands of times before in his life. Curial stepped forward and the old man craned his neck.

"Come to play, or admire my beauty?"

"Maybe a little of both."

The old man clapped his hands together. "Ha, sit down, sit down. I certainly have time to dispatch someone as young as yourself. From the sound of it, you're twelve or thirteen."

"Thirteen," Curial said, taking a seat. "You're good."

"You don't have to tell *me* that," Matthew said, biting on his bottom lip. He reset the clock then tilted his head. "I like to play a quick game, son. Your move. But if you don't mind calling out your move, makes it easier for me to follow the game."

They played for ten minutes, moving fast and furiously. After one particular move, the old man squealed in delight.

"Ooo-wee! I think I see what you're trying to do now. Where you been hiding yourself, boy? You must come down and play more."

"I think I will. I like how you play."

Matthew chuckled and ran his big long hand across his mouth. "And you, son, play just like your mother."

Curial's heart almost stopped.

"My mother?"

"Yes indeed. Now, she played more elegantly than you. You, you're more of a charging bull. But at your core, you play just like her. She obviously taught you well."

Curial gulped. "You knew my mother?"

"I may be blind, but I *know* I don't stutter. That's what I'm telling you." The old man leaned forward and nodded his head. "Yep, you most certainly have her eyes."

Curial felt for his eyes. "How could you possibly know that? Aren't you blind?"

Matthew slapped his own knee and howled. "I love doing that. I know, because she *told* me you had her eyes. She also told me that some day after she was gone, you'd be following a few clues that would lead you right here to me."

"She told you about *me?*"

Matthew nodded. "I knew your mother well. We met years ago at an art gallery, struck up a friendship. She would come down here and play chess. We talked about art, I told her stories, she asked me questions. She was kind, sharp as a whip, funny. Your mother was like the daughter I never had. Her funeral, that was hard on me."

"But I didn't see you at her funeral."

"And I didn't see *you*. Ha! Don't worry, it was a big funeral, and I know how to get around without being noticed."

He stood up, placed his derby hat on his head, and grabbed his cane.

"Walk with me, Curial Diggs."

Curial stood up and came to Matthew's side, the old man expertly maneuvering around tables and chairs as he walked to the main sidewalk. "Yep, your mother and I talked about a great many things. We shared a love of art and a fascination with the disappearance of a particularly fantastic treasure: the Romanov Dolls. And your mother told me that if you ever found me, I was supposed to give you everything we knew about those dolls."

"Are you taking me to where you keep the information?" Curial asked.

"No, I'm just stretching my old bones." He smiled a big toothy grin and pointed to his head. "I keep everything about those dolls right here."

Curial had once heard that blind people often had to rely on memory more than other people, since writing things down was more difficult for them.

"You've remembered *everything* about the dolls?"

"Ha!" Matthew snorted. "Sorry to say that my memory isn't quite what it used to be so I keep the important information on flash drives." He stopped, took his derby off, turned it upside down, and fished his finger into the inside rim of the hat. His forehead tensed up as his hands went to his pockets. "That's weird. It was here this morning." He stopped and cocked his head, then moved it back and forth like he was listening for something. He took two steps off the path towards the trees, then stopped and put both hands on his hips.

"Maurice?" said the old man.

"Did you just say Maurice?" asked Curial.

A chuckle came from deep inside the trees.

"Maurice," said Matthew, "what have I told you about going through my stuff?"

Curial watched the trees move back and forth as a

figure stepped through. It was a kid. A very familiar kid. *This* couldn't be happening. The kid was short, white, and had curly brown hair. He wore blue jeans and a grey hooded sweatshirt.

It was the world's most irritating kid. Maurice. He waved at Curial.

"Well, if it isn't my favorite rich kid."

"Unbelievable," said Curial. He turned to Matthew. "Please tell me you don't know Maurice."

"Know him?" said Matthew, "He's my nephew. Can't you see the resemblance?"

Matthew was tall and black. Maurice was short and white.

Matthew started to laugh. "I took Maurice in a few years ago. Sounds like the two of you have been introduced."

"Unbelievable," said Curial again.

"Sorry Unc," said Maurice, "Curial's just sore because he lost Three Card Monte to me."

"And because he was stalking me in the library earlier today," said Curial.

"Rich kids apparently think they own the library." Maurice shook his head. He held something small, black, and red between his thumb and forefinger and handed it to Matthew. "Your flash drive Matthew, and for the record, I didn't go through your stuff." Maurice smiled. "I lifted it."

Matthew furrowed his brow. "Impossible," he said in a low throaty voice.

Maurice arched his eyebrows. "Are you sure?"

Matthew rubbed his chin with his hand then his eyes grew big. "Coming off the bus, I bumped into a woman carrying her groceries." He held a long finger up in the air. "Well I'll be, an *Old Ruby.*"

Maurice smiled even bigger now.

"An Old Ruby?" said Curial.

Matthew clapped his hands together and howled. "Yes indeed Curial Diggs. You see, an Old Ruby is when the pickpocket positions himself behind or alongside an older woman. Preferably she's carrying groceries or shopping bags. Then, while you gracefully bump her into your target, you use the collision as the opportunity to make the lift."

Maurice straightened his small frame up. "And Uncle Matthew has been telling me that I could never, ever, ever pick and I quote 'the pocket of the master himself.'"

Matthew wagged his finger in the air. "Don't be listening to this fool, Curial, everybody gets lucky sometimes. Now Maurice, give the boy his flash drive."

Maurice held it out and when Curial went to grab it, Maurice jerked it back.

"Got to be faster than that."

Just then, Matthew's cane whacked Maurice in the butt.

"Ouch!" Maurice yelped as Curial grabbed the flash drive out of his hand.

"Forget it Curial," Matthew said. "Maurice has an attitude problem that I haven't yet been able to cure. You take that flash drive home, look through the stuff your mom and I put together, and then come back and play chess with an old man and we'll talk." Matthew smiled, put his derby hat back on, then held his white walking stick out in front of him and walked away. Then he stopped and wheeled around. "Maurice, before you come home, would you mind stopping at Nelsons and buying a bag of black licorice? You know how I like my licorice."

"Sure thing Unc." Maurice put his hand to his jeans pocket, then his eyes grew big as he patted his pockets frantically. He let out a breath. "He didn't."

Up ahead, Matthew chuckled. He was holding a wallet high above his head.

"They call it the *Double Ruby*, Maurice. I Rubied you at the exact moment you Rubied me."

"But, but how?"

Matthew shook his head then pointed to his ears and then his nose. "I heard you coming a mile away. It's your breathing that gives it away. And then, of course, the smell of eleven-year-old boy. I can always smell you coming." Matthew tossed the brown wallet into the air and Maurice caught it. Then Maurice began sniffing his armpits.

"Don't worry Maurice, remember, you're still just a kid." Matthew grabbed some birdseed out of his pocket and threw it on the ground for the pigeons. Then he ambled away.

Curial rolled the flash drive over between his thumb and finger. So his mom really *had* left something for him. Something *big*. His mother had given him so much in his life. And now, when she was gone, she'd found a way to keep giving.

Curial felt a shove in his shoulder. He looked over at Maurice.

"So you're going after the Romanov Dolls, eh?" said Maurice. "I've heard Matthew talk about them before."

"So that whole time in the library about Michelangelo the turtle..."

"Yeah," Maurice smiled. "I actually know about art. Matthew's taught me a ton. The Romanov Dolls are the real deal."

"My mom wants me to find them," said Curial.

Maurice smiled and stood on his tip toes. "Wow! To find those dolls, that's a pretty big job. You're gonna need some help don't you think?" Maurice jabbed a thumb into his own chest.

"You?" said Curial while chuckling.

"Of course me. I know the streets, I help Matthew with his art consulting business—you could use a man like me."

"I could use a man for sure but a boy? How old are you anyway?"

Maurice put both hands on his hips. "Eleven but I'm an old eleven."

Curial looked at him skeptically.

"I'm short okay," said Maurice, "but I can do the work of three twelve-year-olds."

Curial shook his head and started to walk way, then he turned around. "No offense Maurice, really. If I needed to steal somebody's watch, or hustle a kid out of his milk money, you'd be the first person I'd call but this is different." Curial held the flash drive up and looked at it with wonder. "I've got myself a treasure to find."

*_*_*

In the ten minutes it took Mike to rush Curial home, all Curial did was finger that flash drive and wonder what might be on it. For now, Peru would have to wait; the Romanov Dolls were calling.

Mike stopped in front of the Diggs Mansion and Curial raced up the front stoop and flew through the front door and toward the main stairs. Hank yelled after him but Curial ignored his butler, taking the stairs two by two. By the time he pushed open the two big oak doors to the library his breathing was fast and heavy. Didn't matter. He ran through the library toward the spiral staircase.

And that's when he heard a nasaly voice from above. An all too familiar nasaly voice.

Getty stepped from the spiral staircase to the main floor. "What a surprise," Getty said. "You're not in your library working on your studies."

"Is it your mission in life to bother me?" said Curial, as he tried to catch his breath.

Getty sneered. "Sadly, no. Because of my big mouth, you're father's given me a much more unpleasant task."

"What are you talking about?" said Curial.

"When I delivered that folder, I noticed you didn't seem to be paying much attention to school. I mentioned it to your father and told him I thought Haverfield was what you needed. *That* was my mistake."

"Why?" asked Curial.

"Because, instead, he put me in charge of monitoring your studies," said Getty.

Curial's heart began racing. "There's no way dad would make you my tutor."

"That's not entirely true," said Getty as he pulled a large black binder from his leather bag and handed it to Curial. "I have no intention of teaching you." He let out a heavy breath. "But this *is* your new curriculum. Once a month, on the dates listed in the binder, I will come here and test you. I will report the results to your father."

"You've got to be kidding me."

"Believe me, Curial, I wish I was. I don't have time for this."

"Then why are you doing it?" Curial said.

"Because your father is Robert Diggs, I work for him, and he told me to do it."

"It's not your job to babysit me!"

"For once, I agree with you. But here's my problem. One day, when your father hands the company to you, that will make you my boss. And although the prospect gives me nightmares, it's in my best interests that you at least know what you are doing when that time comes."

"But you're not a teacher, you're a banker."

"Curial, please. I graduated in the top ten percent of my class at Harvard and have an MBA from the London School of Economics. I think I'm more than qualified to monitor a thirteen year old smart aleck like yourself."

"I'm not a smart—"

Getty cut him off with his hand. "As I said, I really don't have time for this. Now sit down, so we can get started."

Getty pulled a packet of papers out of his bag and set it on the large table in the center of the library. He set a pen down on top of it.

"But you said you weren't going to be teaching me."

Getty was stone faced. "You're dad insisted on a pre-test. He wanted to know how much you've been slacking off."

"But—"

Getty slashed his hand through the air silencing him once again. "You've got one hour, and if I were you, I'd get focused. Your father does not like to be disappointed so you better do well." Getty said it like a threat.

"Or what?" said Curial.

Getty drummed his fingers on the table. "I hear Haverfield is nice this time of year." Getty picked up the pen and extended it.

"You're out of your mind," said Curial.

Getty shrugged. "Have it your way." Getty pulled his cell phone out and started dialing.

"What are you doing?" asked Curial.

"Calling your dad, of course. I'm sure he won't mind being pulled out of a meeting with the German Chancellor to learn his snot nose kid is throwing a tantrum."

"Wait!" Curial said.

Getty stopped.

"Don't call him. You said I have an hour?"

"I said that a minute and a half ago. If you can do math, then you know how much time you have left."

Curial snatched the pen from Getty's hand, sat down, and began.

CHAPTER EIGHT

SEVEN DAYS

After that horrible test, Getty left, and Curial got to work. He loaded up the files his mom had left for him on Matthew's thumb drive. And that night he tried to learn as much about The Romanov Dolls as he could. He ended up falling asleep in the library, and dreamt of a monster with Godzilla's body, and Getty's face and voice attacking Manhattan, trying to destroy Curial Diggs.

His cell phone woke him up.

Curial picked his head up, wiped drool off his mouth, and reached for his phone.

"Hello," he said groggily.

"I really hope you're tired from all the studying you did last night," said Getty.

Curial was definitely studying, just not what Getty wanted.

"What do you want?" said Curial.

"To tell you that your father almost had a heart attack

when I reported your pre-test score five minutes ago."

"Very funny, how did I do?"

"I actually feel sorry for you. NO, that's not true. It will be delicious to watch your struggle through this. Curial, you did terrible."

"It couldn't have been that bad."

"I'd say a fifty-three percent is pretty bad."

"Fifty-three percent?"

"To be precise, it was a fifty-two and a half percent so I did the generous thing and rounded up."

"I got a fifty-three percent?"

"Yes, Curial, you did and you know what that means?"

Curial was wide awake now, and he was speechless.

"That means in a week and a half, I will test you again and if you don't show dramatic, and I mean dramatic improvement, then—"

"Father will send me to Haverfield," Curial said, his voice a bit shaky.

"Finally," Getty replied, "you got a question right. I'll see you soon." The call disconnected and Curial sat there, stunned, just staring at his phone. Finally, he shivered and stood up. He needed some fresh air.

He spent an hour walking through the park and then finally found himself back at the MAC. He visited his mom's favorite piece, hoping she might have some magical piece of advice for him.

It all seemed so unfair. She had left him a task, an adventure. And just as he'd found it, his dad had found a way to ruin it. He made his way to the renovated main hall, and sat on a newly installed bench in front of the glass enclosure where, very soon, the jewels of the Egyptian Queen Sefronia would be displayed to commemorate the reopening of the exhibit hall.

Curial was just about to leave when he spotted a familiar black coat out of the corner of his eye.

"Hey Claude," he said, a little louder than was probably suitable for the museum.

Claude turned, and when he did, Curial could instantly tell that something was wrong. The curator's shoulders were slumped and he offered only a feeble smile.

"Is something wrong Claude? You look like someone stole your dog."

Claude blew air out through his lips and gently shook his head. "Worse, Mr. Diggs. Much worse." He swallowed, and a lump moved visibly down his throat. "I'm afraid you are looking at the man who will, in just a couple of weeks, be the *former* museum curator of this glorious place."

"W-w-what—what are you talking about?"

"Queen Sefronia's jewels—the ones that I secured from Cairo to open our new hall? The Layton Museum of Chicago snuck in behind my back and negotiated better terms."

"What does that mean?" asked Curial.

"It means our beautiful museum will open without a showpiece, and as a result, the board called an emergency meeting last night. They decided that after the opening, the museum will be forced to go another direction... without me."

The words hung in the quiet museum, Curial trying to make sense of them. He'd known Claude his whole life. His mother had loved Claude.

"But they can't do this."

Claude sighed, his chest and shoulders falling forward. "Yes, Curial, they can."

Curial was in disbelief. Claude was practically a member of the family. Heck, Curial had spent more time with Claude than he had his own father over the years.

"What can I do? Certainly my name still means something around here?"

Claude slowly shook his head. "I'm afraid nothing. The board said it was only because of my relationship with the Diggs family that they kept me in my post as long as they did—but my failure to accumulate 'new and exciting works' was my undoing. Seems the world of art may have passed me by. There was a time when it really was all about the art; but somewhere along the way, acquiring new art became more about politics. In a world of underhanded schemes and backroom deals, I'm probably not what the MAC needs anymore."

Curial's chest was tight and his head spun. His mother would never have let this happen. One call from his father and Claude's job would be safe. But his father would never intervene now. He thought art was a silly diversion.

"I wish there was something we could do," Curial finally managed to say.

"Me too, Mr. Diggs, me too." A worker came by to ask a question, and Claude politely excused himself. Curial sat down and stared at that empty glass case.

Empty. Curial's life had seemed pretty empty without his mother in it. And as he looked around at the big cavernous exhibition hall, he knew that, no matter how much art the next curator found for it, the MAC would seem just as empty without Claude.

Curial kept staring at that glass case, the one that should have been holding the queen's jewels, when suddenly an answer to his problems finally hit him. Getty and his tests would have to wait, even if Haverfield *was* a possibility.

Claude was family.

He looked at that glass case.

Maybe it didn't have to be empty.

There were still seven days left until the reopening of the museum. Seven days to find a piece of art worthy of this grand display case. A piece of art so spectacular that

Claude Von Kerstens would *never* have to leave his job. Studies would have to wait. Curial Diggs needed to find those dolls, and fast.

CHAPTER NINE

TIME FOR A TRIP

Curial found Matthew in the park, described his problem, and started playing chess. After thirty minutes, Matthew howled.

"And that's checkmate," Matthew called as he knocked over Curial's king. "And that game gave me only minor satisfaction because you clearly weren't paying attention."

"Sorry, I'm nervous."

"Listen, Curial. Your mom clearly thought the world of you and I'm sure you can do anything that you put your mind to...but...finding those dolls in less than a week, after they've been gone so long?"

"Needle in a haystack?"

"More like a needle in a Russian countryside full of haystacks."

"But that's just it isn't it? My mom never took the search to Russia before."

"Well, I admire your gumption. And you're sure—"

"I promise to call if something comes up," Curial said.

Matthew stood up and held out his large hand. Curial took it and Matthew wrapped it up in a friendly shake.

"Then there's only one more thing to say. Good luck in Russia."

"Russia," a voice yelled from behind Curial. He turned to see Maurice jogging towards them. "Did I just hear someone's going to Russia? Okay, fill me in on the plan."

"There is no plan," said Curial. "I just need to go to Russia and try and find those dolls."

Maurice clapped his hands. "Fantastic. Never been to Russia myself, should be fun."

"Yeah, right," said Curial. "I'll be going on this trip *alone.*"

Maurice scrunched up his face. "But you don't know anything about that world. You need me."

Curial could see Matthew roll his blind eyes as he sighed. "Maurice, leave the boy alone. Curial's got to do this on his own. God only knows what would happened if I let you go to Russia. You'd probably spend the rest of your days in the gulags."

"But Unc, there's no way Curial can do this by himself. He'll need somebody like me to figure it out."

Matthew put his hand on Maurice's shoulder and squeezed. "Hush now Maurice. I can't have you going to Russia and that's the end of it. Curial, good luck to you and don't hesitate to call."

"Thanks Matthew." Curial waved.

Matthew turned Maurice around and together they walked slowly away. About thirty feet away, Maurice turned back and took one last look at Curial. He looked hurt.

But Curial didn't have time to worry about Maurice's feelings. He needed to finish preparations for the trip. He went over his plan with Hank, had Mike make the necessary travel arrangements and then made his least favorite call in the world.

To Getty.

"Excuse me," the nasaly assistant said. "Did you just say you're going to Russia?"

"Yes Getty for the second time. Father's been encouraging me to take international trips. Mike, Hank, and I made all the necessary arrangements and Mike will be with me every step of the way. Every step."

"Curial, this makes no sense. You did terrible on your test and you'll need every minute of the next week and a half to study for your next test. There's no way I can possibly let you go."

"Listen, Getty. Think about it this way. If I'm not prepared, and don't do well, then like you said, my father will send me on the first train to Haverfield. And when that happens, you'll be rid of me for a very long time."

There was silence on the other end, following by what sounded like the clicking of teeth. "I suppose I could find a way to convince your father."

"I thought you'd come around. I'll be back in seven days and I'll be ready for your stupid test."

CHAPTER TEN

THE GOOD PROFESSOR

During the plane ride from New York to St. Petersburg, Curial ignored the luxury packed into every square inch of the Diggs family's custom-built Gulfstream jet. Instead, he spent his time staring out the window and wondering what, if anything, he would learn about the Romanov Dolls once he got to Russia.

He and Mike arrived in St. Petersburg thirteen hours after leaving New York and left Pulkovo International Airport at 8:15 a.m. local Russian time, with Mike inching their rented blue Volvo through the unfamiliar Russian traffic. All the while Curial craned his neck out the window, getting his first glimpses of the city his mom had always dreamed of visiting.

Curial's first impression of St. Petersburg was that it reminded him a little of Washington, D.C.—just a little dirtier and yet prettier all at the same time. Like D.C., it had no skyscrapers to dominate the skyline, but instead block after block was stuffed with massive four- and five-story buildings. And opposed to the sometimes dreary whites and greys that dominated D.C., to Curial, St. Petersburg seemed like a city unafraid of color. Yellows, greens, reds, and blues dotted buildings all throughout the ride to downtown. Curial had once heard that D.C. had been designed and built to be *impressive*. It seemed to him that St. Petersburg had been built to be *beautiful*.

After checking in at the Four Seasons Hotel, Curial and Mike hustled off to the Diggs Bank of St. Petersburg, where the local bank president, Yefim Posovsky, gave them a personal tour of the operations. Mr. Posovsky used the opportunity as a teachable moment, explaining the differences between U.S. and Russian banking operations, and Curial listened with rapt attention. Well, *fake* rapt attention. As Posovsky droned on about exchange rates, liquidity positions, and market weaknesses, Curial patiently waited for his next move. Eventually Posovsky's tour ended and Curial left the building to find the rented blue Volvo waiting at the curb. The man driving it was now wearing a beret and a scarf. Curial hopped in.

"Nice outfit, Mike."

"I figured I should blend in, really *be* one of the Russian people."

"You look like an extra from a production of *Fiddler on the Roof.*"

"Is it the hat? Is the hat too much?"

"I think it's everything, Mike. Russians don't dress like nineteenth-century Cossacks. They dress more like New Yorkers."

"Sorry, Curial. I did bring flip-flops and my New York Jets jersey, if you'd prefer I wore those."

"Better to stand out than dress offensively."

"That was a cheap shot at my Jets, wasn't it?"

"Just an acknowledgement that you follow the wrong team in New York. But enough about the worst football program in America; I heard some shocking news this morning."

Mike turned in his seat, worry filling his face. "What?"

"I've confirmed with two official sources this morning that St. Petersburg is not at all well known for its hot dog stands."

Mike clutched his heart, then winked while unfolding a map of St. Petersburg. "I'm offended that you would think my gastronomical adventures begin and end with unhealthy pork sausage. I'll have you know that I am a fan of anything with absurd amounts of sugar, fat, or calories of any kind."

Mike's map was covered with red stars.

Curial leaned forward. "What do you have there?"

Mike pointed to one of the stars. "Right here, I've marked all of the best-rated blini and borscht stands throughout St. Petersburg."

Curial's brow scrunched together. "What exactly are blini and borscht?"

Mike shrugged. "I have no idea, except that each is loaded with enough calories to keep people alive in a place that feels like winter nine months out of the year." Mike pointed out the window of the car. "Plus, have you noticed? All the people here are skinny."

Curial smiled. "So that's your plan? Hit twenty or thirty high-calorie Russian food stands in an effort to get skinny?"

"Kind of genius, don't you think?"

Fifteen minutes later, Mike crossed the Neva River to Vasilievsky Island and stopped the car in front of the longest building Curial had ever seen in his life. The three-story building was red with white trimmed windows and white colonnades. It appeared to stretch a block to either side of the center where he stood.

St. Petersburg State University.

"I don't know how long this is going to take," Curial said, "so stay close, okay?"

Mike pointed to the map then motioned down the street. "A block that way, I've got blinis stuffed with whipped cream and strawberries, and the other direction

I have what *International Street Food* calls 'part funnel cake, part vodka, served on a stick.' So don't worry, I won't be far."

Leaving Mike to his dietary excursions, Curial walked toward a large metal statue of an angel. As he did so, an older man with a grey beard, glasses, and a brown tweed coat walked toward him, holding out his hand.

"Valery Ardankin, and you must be young Mr. Diggs."

Curial took his hand. "Curial, please. Did the fact that I'm a kid give it away?"

Ardankin laughed from his belly. "Russia's population is 145 million strong. But less than 100 thousand Russians are black. You tend to stand out."

Curial squinted his eyes and craned his neck. "That's less than one tenth of one percent. I have better odds in midtown Manhattan."

Ardankin walked toward the front door with Curial at his side. "Much better. But don't worry. Most people won't give you problems—you'll just seem exotic to them. Makes blending into Russian society a bit difficult though."

Ardankin stepped inside, leading Curial into an impossibly long hallway that ran the length of the entire building—at least. The floor was wooden and laid out like a chessboard turned diagonally. One side of the hallway was lined with windows to the outside, the other with wooden trophy cases with glass fronts.

"Incredible," Curial said, looking both directions.

"Yes, it is. Peter the Great had twelve buildings built all in a row: twelve buildings to house the twelve branches of government. Eventually all the buildings were connected, and this hallway was born. It helps an old man like me keep his creaky bones limber." He started walking.

"Now, Curial, your family's reputation is great and I know your mother was a wonderful supporter of the arts—but what exactly could you want with an old Russian History professor?"

"I hear you are an expert on the Romanovs?"

"Most people that travel a long way to ask me about the Romanovs don't really care about the Romanovs. Not anymore."

"What do most people care about?"

Ardankin turned, his eyes filled with mystery. "Rasputin."

"The ugly scary guy from the movies?"

Professor Ardankin lifted his fingers and sighed. "Not just ugly and scary. According to the reports, he was a sorcerer, he had an affair with the queen, he was the de facto ruler of Russia... For years, Russians have been fascinated with Grigori Rasputin."

"And not just Russians."

"Yes, the world. Who knows why some figures are so

interesting? So, you are not here to talk about Rasputin?"

"No. I'm here to talk about an object."

A smile formed across Ardankin's mouth. "The matryoshka dolls?"

"Yes, the Romanov Dolls."

Ardankin stopped in front of a door. He inserted a key and pushed it open. "Then we will need a bit of tea."

Ardankin's office looked exactly like what Curial would have guessed an old Russian professor's office would look like. Dark, polished wooden bookshelves covered all four walls, and they were filled with ancient looking, leather-bound books, interrupted only by the occasional painting or artifact. The professor took a kettle off of a hot plate and poured steaming water into two small cups. He brought Curial a cup and handed it to him.

"You haven't had real tea until you've had Russian tea."

Curial sipped and faked a smile. To Curial, tea tasted like cardboard covered in dirt. At best, this Russian tea maybe had slightly fancier dirt.

Professor Ardankin sat in the chair opposite Curial, crossed his legs, and took a long sip of tea. Then he closed his eyes and smiled.

"Tell me, what do you know about the Romanov Dolls?"

Curial looked for a plant where he might dump the tea.

Finding none, he reluctantly took another sip. "Only a little, I'm afraid, but that's why I'm here. You see, my mom used to visit the Manhattan Art Collective when she was a little girl."

Ardankin's eyes lit up and he raised a finger. "Where the Romanov Dolls were mysteriously donated in 1947?"

"Exactly. She loved those dolls—but when she was ten, they were stolen. The rest of her life she was fascinated by their disappearance." Curial looked away from Ardankin into the corner of the room. "She died six months ago."

Ardankin nodded, a somber look on his face. "I'm sorry for your loss."

"I want to know more about those dolls," Curial shrugged, "to keep the memory of my mother alive."

Ardankin pointed his finger at Curial and chewed on his lip. "Or maybe you want to *find* the Romanov Dolls?"

Curial laughed. "Wouldn't *you*?"

Ardankin leaned back and danced his fingers together. "An old man can only dream."

Curial pressed the cup to his lips again, but this time refused to actually sip.

"I've been through all the police reports related to the theft itself and I can't figure out where to go next. My mom thought the answer might lie here, in Russia."

"Why?"

"Well, the only thing we really know about the dolls is

that they belonged to Czar Nicholas II. Then the next we hear of the dolls, they were given to the MAC in 1947. That's a pretty big gap. And my mom, I think she just figured maybe there was more to the story. And maybe, just maybe those dolls found their way back here."

"Ahh, your mom sounds like a smart lady indeed but unfortunately, I don't know much more than you. You are correct, according to the official record, we hear mention of Czar Nicholas II giving a set of dolls of extraordinary beauty to his son Alexei on his fifth birthday."

"He gave a set of dolls to his boy?"

"Not just his boy, the future Czar. After having several girls, Alexei was the one to insure the Royal succession of the Romanov family. As you know, the dolls were magnificent and it makes sense that Nicholas would want a magnificent gift for a boy who was such a gift to him."

"And that's it?"

"Until the dolls showed up at your museum in 1947? I'm afraid that's it. I'm sorry, Mr. Diggs, that you came so far for so little. Is there anything else I can do for you?"

Curial shifted in his seat. He pulled out a sheet of paper with a symbol sketched on it.

"Just one thing and it probably doesn't mean anything. My mom discovered that there was a small symbol etched into the very bottom of the largest of the Romanov Dolls. She

thought maybe it had something to do with who made it. I'm
not sure how it helps but…could you take a look?"

He handed the picture to Ardankin who took the paper
along with a pair of reading glasses. He balanced the
reading glasses on the bridge of his nose while first holding
the paper at a distance, then bringing it closer.

"Do you recognize it?" Curial asked.

Ardankin stared at the paper for another moment then
turned to Curial. He shook his head. "I'm afraid not."

"But do you have any idea what it might mean?"

"I really wouldn't know."

"But it might have something to do with who made it,
right?"

Ardankin glanced at his watch, appeared lost in
thought, then bounced his head back up. "Yes, of course
that's probably it." He stood up. "I am most sorry, Mr.
Diggs, but I just remembered I have another meeting, was
that everything?"

"Yeah, unfortunately. I was just hoping."

Ardankin put a hand on his shoulder. "For answers?" He
sighed. "Sometimes we never find what we're looking for."

"So what would your advice be? Where should I go
next?"

"Have you been to St. Petersburg before?"

Curial shook his head.

"Then you should start with a tour."

CHAPTER ELEVEN

DINA ARDANKIN

Ardankin escorted Curial out of the building and toward the street, where Mike was leaning against the car, examining his food map. As they walked, a beautiful blond girl came directly toward them. She stopped, folded her arms, and glared at Ardankin. Then her face melted into a smile and she threw her arms around the old professor's neck and squeezed tight.

She said something in Russian.

Ardankin squeezed her back, said something else in Russian and then nodded his head at Curial. "In English, little bird, for our guest's sake."

The girl let go of Ardankin, went back to folding her arms, and gave Curial what seemed like an evil eye.

Ardankin stepped back. "Curial Diggs, forgive me, but this is my granddaughter Dina. Dina, this is—"

She stepped past her grandfather and stuck her hand out to Curial. He took it and she squeezed hard like she was trying to crush his hand. Finally she let go, adjusted her ponytail and took a step back.

"You're shorter than I expected."

"Excuse me?"

"Grandfather said he would be meeting the son of a great American, so I googled you." She cocked her head. "Yes, definitely shorter than I expected."

"Is that a good or bad thing?"

She rolled her eyes. "Are you ready, Grandfather?"

He frowned and cleared his throat. "I'm sorry, little bird, but something unexpected has come up, and I need to make some calls."

Her face went blank and her shoulders fell. "But, you—you promised."

"I know, and I'll make it up to you, but it can't be helped today."

"But I thought today was the day."

He squeezed her by the shoulders. "And there will be another day, I promise."

Dina breathed through her nose, her nostrils flaring.

Ardankin looked sideways at Curial and then his eyes twinkled as he touched his chin. "But maybe… Curial, would you like to learn more about the Romanovs?"

"Absolutely."

"Then you need to see St. Petersburg, really *see* it, with an expert guide who can show you all the sights."

Ardankin turned back to Dina and smiled.

Her face went from blank to confused as she looked first at Curial then back to her grandfather. Then all of a sudden, her eyes grew big as saucers and she started shaking her head.

"This is *not* happening," she said, taking a step backward.

"What's not happening?" Curial asked, still not understanding.

"Nobody is more qualified to give you a tour of St. Petersburg than my Dina," said Ardankin. "She's brilliant. And normally"—he arched his eyebrows—"a pleasure to be around."

"Oh," Curial said, looking at the beautiful Russian girl who clearly didn't want any part of this. He felt his face get warm and his palms get sweaty. "Oh! I, er, I totally understand. Don't worry about me at all, Professor, I'll get by fine on my own."

Ardankin put one arm around his granddaughter and laid his other arm around Curial.

"Nonsense. Russians are known for our hospitality—particularly those Russians whose last name is Ardankin." He spit those last words out as if to drive home the point to his granddaughter. "Dina will be happy to help you out, and you will be glad to receive her wisdom."

Curial swallowed hard. "Yes, sir."

Ardankin pulled a handful of Russian paper money from his wallet and handed it to Dina. "This should cover your afternoon. Thank you, little bird." He took her once again into his arms. "And remember, I'll make it up to you."

Ardankin shook Curial's hand, then turned around and walked back into the college, leaving Dina and Curial alone and fidgeting awkwardly for lack of something to say. Dina was looking away from Curial, breathing through her nose so that her nostrils flared. Finally she gave her head an angry shake.

"Yeah," Curial said, not entirely sure how to respond. "Listen, Dina, I've got my driver here. I'm happy you were willing, but I really don't need a tour guide, so you're off the hook, okay?"

"Oh no you don't. If my grandfather found out I let you go off on your own, he'd be furious. Better to just get this over with."

She started walking away from the college. Curial looked over at Mike, who had put down the map and was watching all of this with interest.

"Dina, slow down. I have a driver who can take us. Just tell him where."

She rolled her eyes again. "Typical lazy American. You want to see St. Petersburg? Then for now, you walk. Got it?"

Curial looked to Mike, who just shrugged his

shoulders. "Text me if you need something, okay?" Mike said while folding up his map. "I think my stomach's ready for round three."

Curial looked over to Dina, but she was already half a block away. He ran to catch up, and when he did, she just walked faster. They walked like this in silence for ten minutes when Curial finally stopped.

"Hold up, okay?"

Dina turned and shook her head, then kept going.

"Just hold up," Curial said again. "Why are you in such a hurry?"

She put her hands on her hips. "So I can get this over with, okay?"

"Why do you hate doing this so much?"

Her face tensed up, her jaw muscles twitching. "Because I *should* be with my grandfather. And instead," she waved a hand at Curial, "he makes me babysit a dumb American."

"I'm not dumb, okay?"

"Every American is dumb."

"That's not actually true."

"Wanna bet?"

"Fine."

She pursed her lips and squinted her eyes in a particularly smug look. "Please say something in Russian. Anything you want."

"I don't know any Russian."

A cocky grin crossed her face. "And have you noticed how I've been speaking to you in perfect English this entire time?"

"Well, um—"

"Like I said: dumb American."

She took off again, and Curial hustled to catch up. "Fine, you know my language and I don't know yours. You got me. That doesn't make me dumb."

"Then say something in German, Italian, French. How about Spanish? Surely you must know Spanish?"

"I watched *Dora the Explorer* when I was little; I picked up a few words."

She ran her a hand over her head and tugged on her ponytail. "I know all of those languages, and you don't know any. Not one. Maybe you're not dumb, but like most Americans, you act dumb because you are arrogant and lazy."

"Wait a second: you know six languages? How is that even possible?"

"My grandfather and mother are both university professors. They expect me to follow them in their path. I know languages because I work hard. You should try it."

"You don't know anything about me."

"Like I said, I googled you. You rich kids are all the same. Grandfather told me he had to take a meeting with you because of a generous donation to his department. That's what rich kids do: you throw your money around and think people will do whatever you want."

"I'm not like other rich kids you've known."

"How so?"

"I'm black."

She shook her head. "I don't need the reminder, okay?"

Curial couldn't believe it. "That's pretty racist, don't you think?"

Dina waved her arm around. "Look around, Curial Diggs. Take a good long look. We could walk for the next two hours and never see another black person. How do you think that makes me feel?"

"Like a racist?"

Dina's expression didn't change.

This girl was making Curial nuts. "So you want me to feel sorry for you because you have to be *seen with me*? Listen, at the end of the day, you can go home and never see me again. But I can't change my skin color."

Dina made a strange face. "So the rich American wants *me* to feel sorry for *him* because of the color of his skin."

"I was hoping."

"So you make up for being dumb by trying to be funny."

"I can name the starting quarterback for every team in the National Football League. How's that for dumb?"

Dina looked off to her right and for the first time relaxed her face a little. "I do think Tom Brady's pretty cute."

"You know about Tom Brady?"

A little smile crossed her lips and she nodded. "Boy do I ever."

"Wait a second—so you follow American football?"

"Correction: I follow hot American quarterbacks."

"You know who Peyton Manning is?"

"Never heard of him."

She really did only follow the hot quarterbacks. "Okay, I'll make a deal with you. If I promise to talk about Tom Brady a lot, will you agree not to refer to me as a dumb American?"

"I can only agree not to call you 'the dumbest American of all time.' I reserve the right to call you idiot, moron, or any other applicable term." She gave a slight tilt of her head. "A Russian girl must keep her principles, you know. Now, if you can keep up, maybe this won't be the worst day of my life."

She jogged away and Curial yelled after her. "Got a real gift for flattery, you know that?"

CHAPTER TWELVE

GUNSHOT

Dina gave Curial a tour of the Winter Palace, St. Isaac's Square, and St. Isaac's Cathedral. By the twentieth dumb American joke, Curial was starting to get accustomed to Dina's brand of humor. And one thing was very clear: Dina was not dumb. She appeared to know *everything* about St. Petersburg's most famous sights.

But Curial hadn't yet shared with Dina the real reason for his visit. He was still trying to puzzle it out for himself. Professor Ardankin had only confirmed what little was really known about the Romanov dolls. Curial had hoped that something from the tour would make the picture clearer. Instead, he was as confused as ever.

As they reached a corner, Dina moved ahead of Curial and took a quick right. As Curial came around the corner after her, she grabbed him and pulled him into a small crevice in the wall.

"What the—?"

Dina put a hand on his mouth and held a finger up to her own. Then she pointed out toward the square while the two of them sank deeper into the crevice.

Five seconds later a large man came past wearing a long dark coat, a black derby hat, and carrying a rolled-up newspaper. Dina made eyes at Curial. When the man finally passed, she poked her head out, looked both ways, then grabbed Curial's hand and yanked him out. She hustled away from the man in the dark coat and around the corner, back the way they originally came. One minute of jogging and weaving through cars later, Dina stopped and looked around.

"You ever seen that guy before?" she finally asked.

Curial shook his head. "No, I thought you knew him or something."

Dina stuck her hands in her pockets and scrunched her brow. "He's been following us for the last hour."

Curial gave her a suspicious look.

"I took a few weird detours just to make sure."

"So the exhibit on the *Tooth Care of the Romanov Family* wasn't really your favorite part of the museum?"

She cracked a smile. "I don't like being followed. Must be FSB."

Curial gave her a blank look. "I don't know the FSB."

"Right, your knowledge of Russia comes from bad American movies. You've probably heard of the KGB."

Curial lit up. "Yeah, Russian spies. Kind of like our CIA."

Dina rolled her eyes for the thousandth time. "When the Soviet Union broke up, so did the KGB. Officially. But it reorganized as the FSB. Their people are everywhere."

"And you get followed regularly?"

She frowned and tapped her foot. "Not normally, but my grandfather has taught me to be careful. It must have something to do with you."

"Me?"

She squinted her eyes and rubbed her chin. "They probably think you are an American spy come to steal state secrets."

"How did they even find us?"

"Oh, I don't know. How about asking anybody in St. Petersburg, 'Have you seen a black American kid walking around anywhere?'"

"Is it that obvious I'm American?" Curial asked in fake shock.

Dina laughed, then looked past Curial. Her eyes grew big. "Are you fast?"

Curial spun around. The same man in the dark coat and derby hat was fifty yards away walking quickly their way. Curial turned back; Dina had already taken off.

Curial caught up to Dina and together they jogged for

the next ten minutes, ducking into alleys, weaving in and out of traffic. At one point they even entered a restaurant, walked through the kitchen, and came out the back alley. Eventually they found a taxi and had him take a circuitous route back to the Four Seasons Hotel, where they both got out.

"Okay then," Dina said.

"Yeah," said Curial. "Hey, I'm sorry you didn't get to hang out with your grandfather today."

Her face turned serious again. "Yeah, well, it wasn't horrible. Except for the being followed by the scary man part."

Curial felt bad. He put his hands in his pockets and shifted nervously. "Yeah, about that."

Dina tilted her head and pursed her lips together. "What?"

"It's probably nothing."

"If it was nothing, you wouldn't be acting like this."

"The real reason I'm in Russia…"

"Is not to visit your father's banks."

Curial shook his head. "I'm trying to find something. Something that was very important to my mother." Dina shrugged, and Curial took a deep breath. "The Romanov Dolls."

Dina's eyes lit up and she thrust her head out like an ostrich. "The Romanov Dolls? Oh my God, you're a treasure hunter." She looked up and shook her head. "Now it all makes sense. Why you made a donation to the college to get a meeting with my grandfather. Why you're so fascinated by the Romanovs." She shook her head, her face falling into a frown. "I should have known." She turned around and started walking away.

Curial was confused. He hustled after her and grabbed her by the shoulder. "Wait a minute."

She spun around and knocked his hand away. "You rich Americans are all the same. You come here, throw your money around, and try to take whatever you want. So arrogant—and so predictable. And you know what? The least you could have done was tell me."

She was breathing through her nostrils again, then she turned and walked away.

Curial had no idea what he'd done. Not really. He took the elevator to the fifth floor, walked past three rooms and pulled his key card out.

That's when he noticed it.

The door was cracked open and noise was coming from his room.

Nobody else had a key card to his room.

He thought of the man who followed them around town and he swallowed. He inched toward the door and listened more carefully.

That's when he heard the gunshot.

He pushed the door open and looked into the room.
At who was in the room.

Somebody was about to die.

CHAPTER THIRTEEN

LERGO MY ERGO

The person was small, a video game controller clutched in both hands, grin plastered across his face.

"Hey dude!" Maurice yelled.

"What, where, how—"

Maurice waved Curial off with his left hand.

"Not now, it took me two hours to get to this level."

Curial looked at the television. Maurice was playing a first person shooter game. Two hours? Curial scanned the room. Empty pop bottles lay on the floor. Several empty food plates were spread across the bed. The remote control lay on the floor, sitting in the middle of a not quite empty plate of something brown and gooey.

Curial hit the red button and the TV turned off.

"What?!" Maurice screamed at the TV, his fingers and thumbs still pounding against the controller. Then he looked at Curial "How could you?"

Curial picked up a plate with what looked like half a

hamburger swimming inside of a bowl of mustard. "What the heck is this?"

"Yeah, not nearly as tasty as it looks. I bet myself I couldn't eat a burger completely submerged in mustard. I won that bet. But the good news, with you paying the bill for all this room service, I was actually able to test what I call the lollipop pancake theory."

"Stop talking now. Why are you in Russia?"

"To help you of course," said Maurice.

"I told you not to come."

"And apparently," Maurice winked, "I didn't listen."

"But Matthew let you come anyway?" asked Curial.

Maurice scrunched his face up and looked away.

"Matthew doesn't know? Unbelievable. I don't understand, if Matthew doesn't know, then how did you get here?"

"You really *do* need a partner because you're kind of slow on the uptake. I came with you of course."

Curial shook his head. "Our jet isn't that big. I think I would have seen an annoying eleven year-old riding next to me."

Maurice shrugged. "Then maybe your driver needs to check the luggage more carefully."

"You hid inside our luggage?"

"You act like *you're* the one that's been injured in this whole deal? Do you have any idea how awful it is to ride inside of a tiny luggage compartment on a flight to Russia?"

"I never asked you to come," Curial growled. "In fact, I told you I didn't want you to come."

Maurice dipped his finger into a bowl on the bed and licked it. "And that, Curial Diggs, is the difference between you and me. You *think* you know what you need, but I, being a master of the streets, *know* what you need."

"Oh really." Curial rolled his eyes. "And what is it that I need?"

"Simple," said Maurice. "You need me. Look, I'll prove it to you. You were in Russia all day but without my help. Did you find those dolls? I'll take it by your expression that you did not. Eggo, you need me."

"It's Ergo," said Curial.

"No, I'm quite sure those deliciously perfect waffles I eat every morning are called Eggos."

"Right," said Curial, "but the word you mean is Ergo: it means *therefore.*"

"Now you're just being silly, I eat those golden waffles every day and I think I would know if they were called Ergos. It's not Lergo my Ergo for God sakes."

Curial bit his lip. This was useless.

"Awkward silences are usually good times to turn the TV back on and play video games till our eyes fall out...or should we make a plan for getting those dolls back?"

"What we need to do is call Matthew and let him know

you haven't been kidnapped or killed."

"Do we have to? Usually when I sneak off to foreign countries he ends up yelling at me a lot. I don't like it when he yells."

Curial started dialing. "We talk to Matthew now."

He put the phone on speaker, explained what was going on and then listened. Maurice was right about the yelling.

Lots of yelling.

But when Matthew finally calmed down, he said, "Well Curial, as long as Maurice is there, he might as well help you."

Curial's eyes got big. "Help me? Matthew, you can't be serious."

"Curial, we know finding those dolls is a shot in the dark. Maurice might be a pain, but he's right, he knows the streets."

"Thanks Unc for the vote of encouragement," said Maurice.

"I really just don't want to pay for a ticket to get your lazy bones home Maurice. Curial, you follow the clues you planned to follow, I'll send Maurice to a contact I know on the streets in St. Petes. Let him sniff around, see what he can drum up, what can it hurt?"

Curial scanned the hotel room, the completely destroyed hotel room. He let out a long breath.

"Fine, he can stay."

CHAPTER FOURTEEN

NOT ABOUT THE MONEY

Curial and Maurice left the hotel together.

"So, you heard Matthew," said Curial, "I'll do my thing, and you do your thing."

"I have ears, genius. I heard the same thing."

"Yeah, I just wanted to make sure you understood."

Maurice rolled his eyes. "Listen Curial, by the end of today, I should pretty much have this mystery solved and wrapped up. Don't you worry a bit."

Maurice winked, then pulled his collar up, threw a pair of dark sunglasses on, and hustled away.

Curial shook his head and had the distinct feeling that this was a terrible idea. He looked around and found Mike leaning against the blue Volvo, shoulders slumped, food map nowhere to be seen. "Mike?"

Curial's driver popped his head up and offered a weak smile.

"Something wrong?"

Mike whimpered.

"Are there no more food stands to try in Russia?" asked Curial.

Mike let out a long sigh. "I had a conversation with my wife this morning. She asked if I've been keeping to my diet."

"And like usual, you lied?"

"I couldn't. She said she expected me to come back from Russia thinner than I'd left—or else."

"Or else what?"

Mike got real quiet. Whatever this was, it was serious. "She wouldn't leave you, would she?"

Mike shook his head. "Worse. She said she'd be forced to stop buying Fruity Pebbles. Curial, even on the strictest diets, my wife has always at least afforded me that one small pleasure in life."

"You're joking, right?"

"I wish I was... but I could tell, she wasn't kidding around."

"So you're just going to starve the rest of the trip?"

Mike was getting choked up. "I'm afraid so. And I hadn't even begun to unlock St. Pete's culinary treasures."

This was a problem. Curial had only a few days left to find the Romanov Dolls and he needed Mike at his best.

"I'll make you a deal, Mike. You promise to explore

every food stand on your Russian bucket list and I'll make sure Mabel starts buying Fruity Pebbles for the Diggs kitchen."

Mike looked like a drowning man who'd just been tossed a life preserver. "You'd really do that for me, sir?"

"Trust me, Mike, you do a lot for me. It would be my pleasure."

The color in Mike's cheeks returned, and he looked like he grew six inches. He stepped toward Curial, arms opened. *Dear Lord, he's going to hug me,* Curial thought. Then suddenly, Mike stopped, fake-coughed into his hand, and nodded his head sharply. Curial turned to see what he was looking at.

Standing on the sidewalk, just a few feet away, was Dina.

"You're back?" Curial asked.

"What can I say, I feel sorry for you. The thought of you all by yourself on the streets of St. Petersburg, with people constantly staring at you."

"Again with the black thing?"

She shook her head. "More about the ugly thing."

"You're a real charmer, Dina Ardankin."

"And you weren't honest with me."

"I should have told you."

"And?"

"I'm… sorry?"

"Good." She took out a piece of paper and handed it to Mike. "You want to eat good Russian food? You visit these spots. Tell them Dina sent you."

Curial swore Mike's eyes got a little moist.

"I don't know what to say, Miss."

Dina smiled. "Curial, we've got to assume our friend knows where you're staying. Which means we could use Mike's help before we get started this morning."

Mike shot Curial a confused look.

"It's okay, Mike, not a big deal," Curial said, then turned back to Dina. "What do you have in mind?"

"Misdirection." Dina flipped open her cell phone and made a call in Russian. A minute later she held up her finger. "Okay, there's a taxi waiting for us a few blocks that way." She pointed toward the back of the hotel.

Now it was Curial's turn to be confused. "I don't understand."

"You will. Come on."

Dina and Curial climbed into the back of the Volvo and Mike pulled out, following Dina's directions. They drove in a twisty route for about eight blocks, then stopped in front of a food truck. Dina and Curial got out, ordered a large breakfast, put it in a large white bag, and climbed back into the car. Mike returned them to the hotel, and they went inside with their large white bag.

Once inside, the two kids threw the bag in the trash,

walked straight through the hotel to the back, exited into a back alley, and jogged for two blocks to a yellow taxi that was waiting patiently at the curb.

Dina said something in Russian to the driver as Curial climbed in after her.

"You know what, Dina Ardankin, you're some kind of evil genius, you know that?"

Fifteen minutes later, the taxi driver dropped them off in front of an enormous red stone structure. There was a large iron gate in the middle, and old cannons and guns flanked both sides.

"The Historical Museum of Artillery," Dina said as they walked through the gate. "I figured an American would be interested in a place with a lot of guns."

Curial learned that what was now the Artillery Museum had once been part of the military fortress that Peter the Great had built on the banks of the Neva River in order to defend Russia against Swedish attacks.

When they left the museum they walked along the banks of the Kronverksky Strait until they came to an old wooden bridge. "The Ioannovsky Bridge," Dina said as they walked across toward Zayachy Island, a small island in the middle of the Neva River.

Dina left Curial in the courtyard as she went to get tickets for the different sites. He looked around, taking in the grandeur and beauty of the place. But as old and beautiful and interesting as all of this was, it wasn't getting him any closer to finding the dolls.

"Ouch!" Curial yelped when Dina's fist connected with his shoulder.

"I was talking to you and you didn't even hear me."

"So you *punched* me?"

She smiled and handed him his ticket. "The Peter and Paul Cathedral is up ahead. Come on."

As he walked toward the impossibly tall church spire, Curial still couldn't get his mind off of those dolls and Claude. The reopening of the MAC was in only three days.

"That spire reaches over four hundred feet," Dina was saying. "Tallest thing in St. Petersburg, easily."

Curial's eyes traveled up the spire all the way to the angel on the very top. For a moment, his heart caught in his throat as he imagined the workers installing that sculpture at that height. *Get a grip*, he told himself.

"Can I ask you a question?" Dina said as they stood under the spire and waited in line. "Other than the fact that these dolls are worth a lot of money, why else are they so important to you? I mean, don't you already have enough money?"

Curial hesitated to answer. Telling Professor Ardankin about his mother was one thing; telling this cute girl was something else. He finally let out a long breath. "My mom died six months ago and the dolls were her favorite thing in the world. She left me a note. She wanted me to find those dolls."

Dina took all this in. "So it's not about the money?"

Curial shook his head. "It's about my mom."

CHAPTER FIFTEEN

THE ROMANOVS

As they walked into the cathedral, Curial gasped. The outside of the structure just didn't do justice to how magnificent and beautiful the church was on the inside. Giant marble pillars held up the vaulted ceiling; greens, yellows, and golds adorned everything; fantastic chandeliers hung from above. He thought about how much his mom would have loved to have been there with him at this moment. "This is awesome," he finally said.

"No," Dina said, looking up with him, her mouth in the biggest smile he'd seen on her face. "This is heaven."

They walked in silence down the length of the magnificent church. Finally Curial stopped. "Okay, I told you something; now you tell me something."

She folded her arms and twisted her mouth. "Okay."

"Why were you really so mad yesterday? I can't imagine hanging out with your grandfather is that much fun."

"Why do you want to know?" she said.

"You just seemed more than disappointed, that's all. I figured it must be important."

She looked around and tapped her feet. "My grandfather was going to take me to the St. Petersburg Ballet Theatre, okay?"

"You like ballet?" he asked.

"I love ballet."

"Hmmm."

"What's *that* supposed to mean?"

"I don't know, I just didn't figure you for someone who likes ballet."

Dina's jaw tensed up. "I don't just 'like' ballet. I *am* a ballerina."

Curial laughed out loud, and some tourists turned around and gave him a nasty look. Dina's face was red. "And now you're laughing at me?"

"I'm sorry, the way you make fun of me and hit me, you just don't seem like the ballerina type. You seem... too tough."

"And ballet's not tough?"

"Well, it's just so girly, that's all."

Dina growled and grabbed his arm, then dragged him out of the church and into the courtyard. "You think ballet is girly?" She fixed her ponytail, threw her coat on the ground, stood up on her tiptoes, and put her arms in fixed position.

Curial just watched as Dina started spinning on one toe. Then she hopped straight into the air and kicked her legs out into a full split—and then landed right back down on her tiptoes again. She ran and jumped and spun and kicked, and generally moved the human body in ways Curial hadn't thought possible. Finally she spun one last time, then jumped and landed right in front of Curial.

"Now please, American boy who plays with dolls, I'd love to see you do all those very *girly* moves."

Curial was speechless. "I'm... sorry?"

Dina slipped her jacket back on. "I've studied ballet all my life. Grandfather has connections and was going to introduce me to the director of the ballet theatre so that hopefully I could get a tryout."

"Oh. Well then I *am* sorry."

"Grandfather said we will do it another time, and we will—but I'm tired of waiting. I've waited for too long."

"What do you mean?"

"My mother wants me to be an academic like her and Grandfather, but all I've ever wanted to be is a ballerina."

"And your mom won't let you?"

"Grandfather and I had a plan. Get a tryout with the theatre. And if I was good enough, *then* I would tell Mother. That would show her that I wasn't wasting my time."

"But why don't you just tell her now?"

Dina chewed on her lip. "You don't understand. My mother, she's a very difficult woman."

Actually, Curial did understand.

"Enough about me," Dina said. "Two things left to see in the Cathedral." She pointed toward the entrance. "First thing we do is climb the bell tower."

Curial stopped dead in his tracks. "What did you say?"

"We can't get to the top, but we can go about halfway up. It's really cool."

"I… I can't do that."

"It won't take long, I promise."

"You don't understand." Curial peered nervously up at the spire.

Dina's eyes grew with recognition. "I see, you're scared."

"I'm not—well, yeah… I am."

"So how about you never call ballet girly again, okay?'

"Okay. Then what else is there to see?"

Dina smiled. "The Romanovs, of course."

They walked to St. Catherine's Chapel, and Dina pointed to the tombs set into the walls. Curial stepped up to the first one and ran his hands along it. Supposedly, the Romanovs were buried just a few inches from his fingers. And then something clicked. Could it be that easy?

He spun around. "So they're really buried behind these walls?"

Dina shrugged. "What's left of them. The remains weren't always buried here. In fact, no one had the slightest idea *where* they were buried until 1991, when someone discovered the bodies in a grave near Yekaterinburg. After scientists used DNA testing to identify them as the Romanovs, they re-buried them here in 1998."

Running his fingers over the ornate plaques, Curial walked from Nicholas all the way through the rest of the family, puzzling through his idea. Dina read the Russian attached to each plaque as he went.

"And there is Anastasia," Dina said, as Curial reached the last one. "She was always my favorite."

"She's everybody's favorite. But where are the others? I only count five members of the family. That leaves Maria and Alexei."

Dina shrugged. "Why does it matter?"

"Why does it matter?" Curial asked, his voice cracking. "Because these—these are the Romanovs, and they're not all here. Plus, I have a theory."

"A theory?"

"An idea. Nobody has ever had a good explanation for how or why the Romanov Dolls were taken, but I think... just maybe."

"And would you like to share your brilliant theory with me?"

"If you promise not to make fun of me."

Dina remained stone-faced.

"I'll take that as yes, you will absolutely make fun of me."

She nodded.

"I've read a lot about ancient civilizations. And when someone died in those civilizations, especially someone important, it was pretty common for them to be buried with objects that were special to that person. I have a hunch that royal families function similarly. But when it comes to the Romanovs, things are different, because they were murdered—and whoever murdered them certainly wouldn't have shown them great care in burying them."

Dina's face was flooded with confusion. "Not sure I see where you're going."

"Well, the Romanov Dolls were spectacular, and they belonged to Alexei—given to him on his fifth birthday. That would be *exactly* the kind of object someone would want to send with the boy on his journey to the great beyond."

"The great beyond?"

Curial started pacing and hitting his hand with his other fist. "Yeah, think about it. For over seventy years, from 1918 to 1991, nobody knew where the Romanovs' bodies had been buried. Maybe someone had the dolls, and *wanted* to bury the dolls with Alexei, but couldn't—

and so they hid the dolls until Alexei's body could be found."

"If that's the case, then why were the dolls given to your museum?"

Curial scrunched his face. "I don't know. Maybe whoever had the dolls got anxious, figured the bodies would never be found, and wanted to share the treasure with the world?"

"Okay, then why were they stolen again years later?"

"I don't know that either. Maybe whoever gave them to the museum changed their mind? Or maybe somebody *else* wanted to save the dolls for when the bodies *were* found."

Dina blew out a big breath and shook her head like she had a shiver. "So what you're saying is, you think someone stole the Romanov Dolls from the museum in order to bury them with Alexei's body—to help him on his journey through the afterlife?"

Curial nodded.

"And you believe the dolls are, right now, buried with Alexei?"

Curial thought it over again. Yep. It made perfect sense. This great treasure was indeed *buried* treasure. He pointed at Dina. "Admit it. My theory works."

Dina smiled. "It does work, at least a little. There's just one small problem."

DANIEL KENNEY

"Which is?"

"Maria and Alexei aren't buried here."

"Obviously. Which room are they buried in?"

Dina shook her head. "You don't understand. Maria and Alexei aren't buried *anywhere*."

Curial stopped breathing. "I don't—"

"Understand. Yes, clearly. Like I said, these Romanovs' remains were discovered near Yekaterinburg in 1991— but Alexei's body wasn't among those found. It wasn't until 2007 that Alexei's remains were uncovered, along with the remains of Maria, one of his sisters."

"So, okay… but why haven't Alexei and his sister been buried with the rest of them?"

Dina sighed. "There is… some controversy. You see, many people don't believe these bones—or the ones found in 2007—really belong to the Romanovs. The Roman Orthodox Church in particular. The Church still does not recognize the remains."

"Why not?"

"It's a delicate matter for the Church. To the Church, the Romanov family died as martyrs of the faith, and thus are saints. And in the Church, there is a tradition of venerating the 'relics' of a saint: their bones. And, well…"

It hit Curial like a truck. "The Church wants to be extra careful that people don't venerate the wrong bones."

"Exactly. So when these Romanov bodies were buried

in 1998, it was a huge deal and source of embarrassment that the Church wouldn't recognize the remains. Because of that, when the remains of Maria and Alexi were discovered in 2007, the authorities decided to be much more careful and deliberate about identifying them—and things are just taking their time."

"So… what, the remains are just sitting in a box somewhere?"

"Scientists have them, I guess. I don't really know."

"Could you find out?"

"Grandfather could find out, I suppose. But why does it matter? It's not like the dolls are just sitting on a lab table next to the bones."

Curial's face fell. He looked down at his watch, thinking about Claude. Less than three days.

He needed another theory, and fast.

CHAPTER SIXTEEN

THE DOLL SHOP

"My mom wanted me to come to Russia to find out the truth about the dolls. She wanted me to start at the beginning. But so far…"

"So far," Dina said, "you've come to St. Petersburg, where your mother dreamed of you going."

"Yeah, but I haven't found the dolls."

"Curial, you're *not* going to find the dolls. Whoever has them doesn't want them to be found."

Curial looked at Dina, then twisted his face and looked down at the ground.

"I can't accept that. Somebody's got to know something about these dolls. Something that can help us." He chewed on his lip. "According to your grandfather, the dolls were given to Alexei Romanov in 1909 and that's it…as far as the historical record goes. But what about the dolls themselves? About how they were made? Do you think I could find anyone who might know more about how the dolls were made? Is there any place that still sells matryoshka dolls?"

Dina laughed. "Only about a thousand places."

"Any place you can think of where they still *make* matryoshka dolls?"

"For the record, a girl being into ballet is much better than a boy being into dolls."

Curial ignored the jab. "Do you know of any place?"

"Yeah," Dina said. "I do."

Thirty minutes of walking later, they were standing in front of a store decorated with a yellow and green wooden sign that hung from metal hooks.

"In English it would be called 'Dolls of Beauty,'" Dina said. "No finer place in St. Petersburg for a boy to look at dolls."

She pushed the door open and a bell clanked against the glass. Curial followed her inside.

The store was circular, maybe twenty feet across. Its floors were made of old wooden planks with spaces between them; Curial felt like the floor might tilt a little downhill. And surrounding the circular space on all sides were shelves upon shelves of painted wooden dolls. Some were matryoshka dolls, others were small sculpted dolls similar in size to a Barbie. Still others looked like puppets, with strings and sticks sticking out of their backs.

Curial stared. "This place is—"

"Amazing, I know. When I was little I came in here all the time with Grandfather."

A small woman with short chestnut brown hair and glasses walked in from the back. She leaned her forearms onto the counter and began to say something in Russian, and then her eyes grew big as plates. She laughed, then jogged around the counter and opened up her arms.

Dina stood on her tippy toes, stretched as tall as she could, and smiled widely.

The woman squeezed Dina tightly, said something in Russian, then backed away, her face suddenly cross. Dina responded in Russian, but then pointed to Curial and said "English." The small woman's eyes grew big. She switched to a heavily accented English.

"Explain yourself, young lady, it has been far too long. Why do you not visit me anymore?"

Dina turned to Curial, an embarrassed look on her face. The woman turned to Curial too, her face turning from cross to stern.

"And who is this boy?" She studied Curial for a moment then sidled up next to Dina and grabbed her hand. "This boy giving you trouble, is he? Is he the reason I haven't seen you in months?"

Dina pushed the woman's hand away. "Yes, Valeeni, it is true. I have been kidnapped by this boy and he has kept me away from doll shops until today."

The woman cracked a smile and shook her head. "You make fun of an old woman and think it's funny?"

Dina reacted in mock surprise. "I would never dream of making fun of an old woman! Although I love teasing a beautiful young girl such as yourself."

The small woman blushed and Dina put her arm around her.

"No, Valeeni, I am afraid that I and my laziness are completely to blame for my absence. I am sorry." She kissed the woman on the top of the head and the woman pushed her away, laughing.

Dina gestured to Curial. "And this is my friend Curial. He is American."

Valeeni spoke out of the corner of her mouth. "And very black."

Curial laughed.

"Valeeni, my friend here is in great need of some Russian culture, and he would like to know more about matryoshka dolls."

Curial raised a finger. "Specifically, the Romanov Dolls."

The small woman screwed herself up and practically grew two inches. She skipped across the showroom floor and settled on a set of nested dolls halfway up a shelf.

"The most beautiful matryoshka dolls in all of Russia can be found in our shop—and as for Romanov dolls, we have several different selections. This one, for instance, starts with Catherine the Great and ends with Nicholas II, while this one—"

Dina put her hand on the woman's shoulder and squeezed.

"No, Valeeni. He wants to know more about *the* Romanov Dolls."

The woman cleared her throat. "*The* Romanov Dolls?" Valeeni glanced at Dina who nodded, then turned toward Curial.

He spoke up. "The ones given to Alexei on his fifth birthday. The ones that showed up in 1947 at the Manhattan Art Collective, and the ones that disappeared in a famous art heist twenty-three years later."

"Yes, *those* Romanov Dolls," the woman said, chewing on the end of her glasses and nodding gravely to herself. Finally she took the glasses out of her mouth and pointed them at Curial. "Just who exactly are you?"

"Like Dina said, an American desperately in need of some Russian culture."

"Then to learn about *the* Romanov Dolls, you must come with me."

CHAPTER SEVENTEEN

SPECIAL SYMBOL

Dina and Curial followed Valeeni behind the counter, through a doorway, and along a small corridor that slanted downward. They followed the creaking floor back into a workshop, where an old man sat on a stool, busily painting a set of matryoshka dolls.

"Gennady?" the small woman said.

The old man didn't budge, just kept painting away as if Curial and Dina didn't exist.

"Gennady!" The small woman yelled this time, stomping her foot against the creaky floorboards as she did.

The old man turned and lifted a white earbud from his left ear.

Valeeni said something in Russian and an annoyed look came over the man's face.

"Can't it wait, woman? Miley was just coming in like a wrecking ball."

Curial exchanged a look with Dina.

"Miley Cyrus?" Curial asked.

Valeeni's face was two shades of pink and she shook her head. "My Gennady is obsessed with Miley Cyrus— much to my everlasting shame."

"I've followed her ever since her *Hannah Montana* days," Gennady said, fully turning around now and removing both earbuds. "I knew she had genius in her even back then. Guess who was right, dear?"

Valeeni turned completely away from her husband while he playfully stuck out his tongue at her. He then gingerly walked over to Dina and held his arms out.

"Come give your Gennady a hug and I won't make any comments about how you never come to visit us anymore."

"I think you just did."

The old man winked at Curial. "I'm sneaky that way."

Then he turned toward Curial and held out his hand. "You are black."

"So I keep being told. My name is Curial."

"And you're American?"

"Dina refers to me as a dumb blockhead American."

The man let out a belly laugh.

"Gennady," Dina said, "Curial is a friend of my grandfather and I have been asked to show him around St. Petersburg."

Valeeni stepped between Dina and Gennady. "He wants to know more about the Romanov Dolls."

"Well we have a good selection out—"

"No, husband. *The* Romanov Dolls."

"Oh." Gennady nodded his head and took a few breaths. "*The* Romanov Dolls. Well. In that case, you know what we need? Chocolate. Sipping chocolate, to be clear, like drinking a candy bar. My Valeeni, her sipping chocolate is the second grandest thing in all of Russia."

Valeeni put one fist against her hip. "And what is grander?"

Gennady squeezed her hip playfully. "You are, my dear, you are."

Valeeni's face once again turned two shades of pink, and she walked away.

Gennady looked after his wife, shook his head, and returned to his workbench. He picked up an iPod and placed it in a port with speakers.

"Okay. Miley? Taylor Swift? Lady Gaga? What does my American friend want to listen to?"

"I was hoping I would just listen to you."

"Good answer. So what is it you would like to know about the Romanov Dolls?" He gestured to a pair of small stools, and Dina and Curial both took a seat.

Curial shrugged. "Professor Ardankin just verified what I already knew, that the dolls were stunning and that they were given to Alexei Romanov for his fifth birthday. But I was wondering, do you know anything about how the dolls were made? I assume part of why they were worth so much is that, according to my mom, nobody could figure how the dolls had been made so perfect. Especially since most matryoshkas are crafted out of wood, not precious metals and fine jewels."

Gennady's eyes did something funny—but just for a moment, and then it was gone. He turned to the sound of Valeeni walking down the corridor, bringing a silver platter with her. She handed a small silver cup to Gennady and one each to Dina and Curial, before sitting in a rocking chair in the corner.

"So you want to know how the Romanov Dolls were made, eh?"

Curial took a taste of his sipping chocolate, and turned to Valeeni. "This is delicious. Thank you." He turned back to Gennady. "Do you have any ideas?"

Curial watched Gennady as he took a long drink of his own sipping chocolate, his eyes taking a sideways glance toward Valeeni, who seemed to be chewing on the inside of her mouth while she rocked. Finally, Gennady pressed his lips together and shook his head.

"A great mystery among toymakers, I'm afraid."

Gennady rubbed his hand across his mouth.

"And that's it? That's your best guess?"

Gennady leaned forward and gestured with his finger.

"If you want my guess? My guess is that there was a team of artists working on those dolls for years—and when the dolls were finally perfect, they gave them to Czar Nicholas. *That,* I believe, is the true story."

Curial considered this. "I was reading about the history of matryoskha dolls, that the first dolls were carved in 1890 by Vasily Zvyozdochkin (ZV-YOZ-DOACH-KEEN) and I was thinking that must have made him very famous. And I guess I was guessing that if Czar Nicholas wanted someone to make a special set of dolls for him, who better than the most famous doll maker in Russia. Do you think it's possible that Zvyozdochkin (ZV-YOZ-DOACH-KEEN) made the Romanov Dolls?"

Gennady took another long sip. "I really don't know but as I said, my guess is that a team of artists made those dolls."

Curial thought a moment. "Well then do you know if there are any relatives of Vasily Zvyozdochkin who are still making matryoshka dolls?"

Gennady quickly grabbed a doll and started painting again. "I wouldn't really know, but none that are famous. Valeeni and I know all the famous ones, don't we dear?"

Valeeni nodded, her hands folded in her lap.

Things lapsed into an awkward silence then, with Gennady returning to his work and Dina and Curial sipping their chocolates. When Curial finished his, he stirred the bottom with his spoon and licked the end of the spoon, trying to savor every last drop. "That really was delicious, Valeeni, thank you so much."

Finally, Curial shrugged at Dina and stood. "And thank you Valeeni, Gennady for your time."

"Anything for a friend of our Dina. Now, do not be a stranger anymore," Valeeni said to Dina, while grabbing her and squeezing her again.

"I promise."

Gennady waved to them both and Valeeni escorted the two out of the shop. As they left, the little bell clanked against the glass.

They were both quiet as they walked down the sidewalk. Finally, Dina punched Curial in the shoulder.

"Ow!"

"What exactly is going on here, Curial?"

"I think you just punched me in the arm again."

"No, with Gennady and Valeeni. They weren't acting normal."

"How so?"

"They were—I don't know—they were being weird."

Curial's body tensed as he noticed someone moving toward them on the sidewalk.

"Oh crap."

"I know, I can't figure out why they were acting so weird."

"No Dina, the big guy in the dark coat, he found us."

Dina spun just as the large man picked up his pace. He wasn't even trying to hide it. He was coming their way.

Together, they turned the opposite direction and started to quickly walk away. A small blind man crossed their path. He stopped and lifted up his sunglasses.

Correction. It wasn't a man.

"Maurice?" Curial said.

"You can thank me later Curial. Just keep moving and don't turn around. I assume the large man in the trench coat is the one who's been following you?"

Dina spun around. The big buy was thirty yards away.

"I said don't turn around," Maurice hissed. "We need to hustle if we're going to make it on time and lose this guy."

"Why are you here?" said Curial.

"Because maybe I knew my best friend would need some help."

"I'm not your friend."

"Just keep telling yourself that rich kid."

Dina was confused. "You two know each other?"

Maurice whacked his walking cane against the concrete. "Move it lovebirds, we don't have time for the chit-chat."

"And where exactly are we going?" Curial asked after following Maurice across the street.

Maurice's eyes looked past Curial. "That big guy can really move. If you must know, we're going to Moscow."

"Moscow!?" Dina and Curial both said in unison.

Curial grabbed him by the shirt and stopped him. "Maurice, what is going on?"

"I told you I'd have this whole thing wrapped up today. While you and blondie here were sightseeing all day, I've been running down the only clue we have."

"What are you talking about?"

"The etching in the bottom of the doll, I figured out what it is, and that's why we're going to Moscow."

Maurice motioned for them to follow and then he sprinted across another street. He pointed in the distance at the train station.

"Maurice!" yelled Curial.

Maurice looked around nervously. "I don't have time to explain."

Curial stood firm and folded his arms. "And I'm not going to Moscow unless you do explain."

Dina shook her head in frustration. "And I'm not going to Moscow at all."

Maurice looked at his watch impatiently. "Listen, have you seen *Indiana Jones*?"

Curial managed a half-smile. "Only the greatest movie ever made."

"In the movie, the German Nazis are trying to find the

Ark of the Covenant because Hitler believes the ark has special powers that he can harness as some kind of super weapon. Well guess what? After Stalin learned about Hitler's program, he decided to get into the act too. He created a top secret program to find artifacts with special powers. Just like the Nazis had the special symbol, the swastika, Stalin's program had a special symbol."

Dina's face suddenly grew curious. "The etching on the bottom of the Romanov Dolls?"

"Exactly," said Maurice.

"Maurice, you found all that out today?" Curial asked.

"Don't look so surprised. Like I've been saying, you need my help. Now come on, the train leaves soon."

Maurice started to jog away when Curial caught him by the arm. "Wait Maurice. Why Moscow?"

"Man you're needy. Because I also figured out who ran that top secret organization."

"You did?"

Maurice's eyes suddenly grew big. "Oh crap, I think big trench coat guy brought some friends with him."

From one direction, the big man in the trench coat continued his gradual march toward them. From the other, three tough looking men came toward them, walking shoulder to shoulder.

Dina grabbed Curial and pulled him hard. "We need to go now!" The three of them broke into a sprint and as soon as they did, Curial could see the three men beginning to run as well.

Dina was in the lead, weaving in and out of the foot traffic as crowds of people marched toward the train station.

"Please tell me you already bought the tickets!" yelled Dina from ahead.

Maurice laughed. "What would you do without me? Of course I have the tickets."

Just then a man jumped in front of Dina with his arms wide open and growled. She hit the ground, rolled under his arms, bounced up and kept running.

The man regrouped and came straight at Curial. Curial tried to move around him but the man was too fast, his arms grabbed onto Curial from the side. The man barked something in Russian as Curial tried to squirm away, then all of a sudden the man's body went limp and he screamed.

Maurice has whacked him in the back of the legs with his walking cane.

"Thanks Maurice, I owe you one."

Maurice slapped the tickets into his hand. "You get up there with Dina and get our seats, I'll create a diversion."

Curial grabbed Maurice and dragged him along. "How about we forget the diversion and both get on the train?"

They sprinted. Half a block away, Dina was at the steps

of the train, waving for them.

Curial turned around. The three men were almost on them.

"Oh crap."

As if by instinct, Maurice stopped and started violently swinging his walking stick back and forth. The men immediately stopped their pursuit.

"Go Curial, go!" Maurice yelled.

Curial sprinted ahead and handed the attendant their tickets. Then he and Dina jumped on. The train started to slowly move.

"Maurice!" Curial yelled.

Maurice threw the cane at the men and screamed, then spun around and made a dead sprint for the train. Son of a gun, Curial thought. He was going to make it. He might be annoying as heck, but this Maurice, he was also pretty brave.

"Come on Maurice!" Dina yelled.

The train was moving faster now and the attendant told Dina and Curial to take their seats but Curial was focused on Maurice. He was just ten feet away now, and Curial reached his hand down.

"Now Maurice, jump now!"

Then Maurice jumped just as a man flew in from the right and grabbed him in mid-air.

"No!" Curial yelled. But it was too late. The man had

Maurice, who was kicking and swinging his arms and screaming. The train was speeding up now and all Curial and Dina could do was watch as Maurice quickly faded into the distance.

CHAPTER EIGHTEEN

MOSCOW

Curial stumbled as the train surged forward. As he steadied himself, he saw Dina looking around as if trying to get her bearings.

"We need to get off this train," Curial said.

Dina breathed in through her nose, then shook her head. "First stop is an hour away."

"Then we get off in an hour, come back to St. Petersburg, and find Maurice."

Dina shook her head again. "There are over five million people in St. Petersburg. How exactly do we find him?"

"I don't know, we call the police."

"We are not in America. For all we know it's the police who took him."

Curial became aware that people on the train were staring at him, and Dina was already walking down the aisle towards empty seats. She sat down and moved towards the window. Curial sat next to her.

"Then we call your grandfather. He's an important man at the University, he could help us out right?"

"There is no way I'm telling my grandfather that I've gotten myself mixed up in…whatever this is. You're the rich American, why don't you call someone?"

"I would also rather not tell anybody what I've gotten mixed up in."

"So it appears we're at a standstill."

"Yeah," Curial said. "It does."

"Then listen. Maurice was telling us he figured something out about that symbol."

Curial pulled a piece of paper out of his pocket and opened it up. "He said it was a symbol of a secret KGB program and that he'd figured out who ran the program and the answer was in Moscow."

"And I'm guessing this guy heard Maurice was poking around in his business and had his guys take him. Which means…"

"We go to Moscow and figure out who this guy is."

Dina seemed to think about it for a moment, then finally nodded. "It's our best shot. We find that guy, maybe we find your friend."

"He's not my friend."

"So he just saved your life back there because he's not your friend?"

Curial looked away. "How long does it take to get to Moscow?"

"On this train? Only four hours."

"Is that enough time to come up with a plan?"

Dina bit her lip. "Don't worry blockhead, I've already got one."

*_*_*

After Curial and Dina arrived in Moscow three hours and forty-five minutes later, they took a cab driven by a man who thought stopping meant slowing down just enough so passengers could jump out without killing themselves.

Curial avoided a car and followed Dina onto a circular berm in the middle of the square. They stared at the front of a massive building. Five stories tall, windows and colonnades filling up every square inch, the stone a light brown with reddish hues.

"Lubyanka," Dina said menacingly. "The headquarters for the Russian secret police. First the Cheka, then KGB, and now FSB. But always the same."

"And we're just going to walk in the headquarters of the FSB and ask for their help?"

"No," she pointed down the block. "Thankfully, there is a museum down there which is much less scary."

Dina led Curial a block away to a fairly dilapidated building. On one corner was a grocery store. On the other end was a broken down building, with plywood covering the windows. In between, was a door with the number twelve in large black letters.

Curial frowned. "That's a museum?"

"A very small museum."

His frown worsened. "A very ugly museum."

"You expected Russian secret police to have a pretty museum?"

Dina took the door and opened it, a buzzer sounding as Curial followed her in.

The museum was definitely not pretty. To the contrary, it was the smallest and least glamorous museum Curial had ever seen. Like what a museum for 1970's office equipment might look like. As Dina walked towards a woman at the front desk, Curial scanned the room, dust and old carpet fogging his view.

"May I help you?" The tall, middle-aged woman said as she looked up from her computer screen. Her eyes fell upon Dina, then opened wide as they danced over to Curial. Her mouth fell open slightly, then she shook her head a bit and returned to Dina.

"You are interested in a tour of our museum?" She stepped to the side and offered her arm as if she was about to start a tour. A tour of what Curial had calculated was a room no larger than twenty by thirty feet. It was a wonder the Louvre was better known than the FSB Museum.

"Sorry," Dina said. "No tour today."

The woman's eyebrows slumped.

Dina stepped forward. "We are doing some research, and thought you might be able to provide some answers."

The woman folded her arms. "What kind of research?"

Dina took out the piece of paper with the symbol. She handed it to the woman. "We wondered if you might recognize this symbol."

The woman glanced at it, then arched her eyebrows and looked at Dina and Curial over her glasses.

She waved the paper in the air. "Where did you get this?"

Dina exchanged a nervous look with Curial.

"My grandfather," said Dina.

"And where did your grandfather get this?"

Dina shrugged. "I don't know. He was in the war and this was with his things. When I was little, I found it, and he told me it was a symbol painted on the bottom of a very important object. That there was a special group in the Soviet Army that went around collecting objects that had special powers."

"Special powers?"

"That's what my grandfather told me. Anyways, he's gone now, and, I've always wanted to learn more. Was my grandfather's story the truth?"

The woman seemed to stand a little straighter, then she

looked at the symbol and at Dina and Curial again. Finally, she cocked her head a bit and took off her glasses.

"There was a group but it wasn't in the army, which I'm guessing you already knew since you're here at the FSB museum, no? Stalin heard about Hitler's plans to collect objects, special objects, and so he formed his own group, a special part of the secret police. The group had their own symbol." She shook the paper. "*This* symbol. And they imprinted it on the objects they found."

Dina turned to Curial and they shared a smile.

"And the two of you are looking for one of these objects, no?"

Dina stood taller. "The program, the special program, who was in charge of it?"

"His name was Koralenko, Anton Koralenko. One of the very few trusted confidents that Stalin did not have murdered."

"So he's still alive?"

She laughed. "No, Anton Koralenko is not alive."

Curial's shoulders fell.

She handed the paper back to Dina. "But his son Victor is. Victor Koralenko is a very important man, former KGB himself."

Dina put the paper back in her pocket. "You said former, what does he do now?"

The woman smiled and lifted her hands up in the air.

"Victor Koralenko does art now. He's one of the great private collectors in all of Russia. His home is practically a museum itself." She studied Dina and Curial again. "You want to tell me what object you are looking for?"

Curial stepped forward but Dina caught him by the elbow and squeezed. Then she took a step back.

"No, thank you. I think we learned what we needed."

The woman's eyes danced, then she held up a long bony finger. "No please, wait. I know someone who can help you." She walked a few steps and grabbed a phone from the wall.

Dina leaned in. "We need to go now Curial."

"But shouldn't we let her help us first."

"I don't think she's trying to help us."

The woman's eyes grew big. She pointed a long finger at them.

Dina hissed. "We need to go now."

Curial followed Dina as she pushed the door open and sprinted away from building number twelve, a tall bony woman screaming Russian behind them.

CHAPTER NINETEEN

RED SQUARE

"I told you this was a bad idea," Curial yelled ahead to Dina. Off to his right a black car stopped and two men jumped out. The woman kept screaming in Russian.

The men started running as Curial caught up to Dina. "I assume you have a plan for how to get out of this?"

Curial spun around to take a look. The men were twenty yards behind and closing fast.

"You could just throw money at them and try to buy them off." Dina stopped and pointed across the street. "There!" She jumped in front of an oncoming car and held up her hands. The car skidded to a stop while blaring it's horn. Dina ignored it and weaved her way through the mid-day traffic, Curial close behind. She hopped onto a red scooter and hit the gas. She turned to Curial. "Well hop on!"

Curial looked behind him. One of the men was crossing the traffic, coming for them. Curial hopped on the back of the scooter and wrapped his arms around Dina's waist.

"You're stealing someone's motor scooter?"

"I'm happy to leave it here if you'd rather we visit with those nice FSB agents."

Dina revved up the scooter and that's when Curial noticed the next problem. Dina was facing towards oncoming traffic.

"What exactly are you doing?" He yelled as she pulled out into traffic and sped away.

"It's called saving your blockhead, now shut-up and let me drive!"

She swerved to the left of an oncoming car, then squeezed in between two taxis.

"Oh my God, oh my God, oh my God!"

"You worry too much," Dina practically cackled.

For one fantastically scary block, Dina swerved in and out of oncoming traffic, then suddenly took a sharp right so they were now going with traffic, the correct direction.

Curial let out a huge breath. "Thank you for not killing me."

Dina swiveled her head.

"Don't thank me yet, we're being followed."

Curial spun in time to see a black sedan take a left onto their same street and speed off after them.

"Crap."

He felt the scooter surge forward as Dina increased the speed. He tightened his grip around her waist. She took a sharp left which Curial wasn't expecting. His body leaned over to the right but he hung on tight.

"Maybe warn me the next time?" he said.

"Sorry, didn't know I was turning until the last second."

Dina sped down what looked like a connecting street and Curial heard the roar of the sedan getting closer.

Dina took a right in front of an oncoming truck then changed lanes immediately. In front of them, the street opened up for several blocks. She gunned the engine. She squeezed in between four sets of cars and each time she did Curial felt like a nut going through a nut cracker. But the roar of that black sedan faded into the distance and Curial suddenly felt like they just might get out of this.

Until he noticed Dina slowing down.

"Wait, what are you doing?"

She drove up onto a sidewalk and stopped the scooter next to a newsstand. She climbed off. "They will be looking for a scooter. Now we go on foot."

"And how exactly are we supposed to outrun them on foot?"

Dina pointed ahead to what looked like a dead end, people walking towards something."

"We're not going to outrun them, we'll outthink them.

Up ahead is Red Square and at this time of day, they'll be a couple thousand people milling about. We get lost in the crowd and find another way out of here."

Dina sped her walk up to a skip and Curial followed. Before he knew it, they had crossed a street and joined a group of people in front of a beautiful red church that looked like a cross between a church and a palace.

"The state historical society," Dina pointed out as if by habit.

Curial looked on in wonder. "Now that, *that* looks like a museum."

She grabbed his hand. "Come on."

She pulled him into a crowd of people filing into Red Square. On their left was an enormous building that really did look like a palace, one that might continue forever. On the right side was a long red wall with an equally impressive building peeking out from behind.

"*That*," Dina said while pointing to their right. "That is the Kremlin wall, and behind it is the Russian President's official residence. All the main functions of Government take place inside the Kremlin walls."

Curial pointed to their left. "And what's that enormous building?"

"GUM." Dina said plainly.

"No, I asked about the building."

She rolled her eyes. "I know, it's called GUM, it's a

Russian acronym that you wouldn't understand because you of course don't know Russian. Basically, that building is the largest shopping mall in Russia."

"It looks too old and fancy to be a shopping mall."

"Let's just say it was the first shopping mall. Now please hurry."

She pulled them forward when the crowd in front of them suddenly parted and another building came into view. Curial stopped and opened his mouth. A building like no other in the world. Shaped like the flames of a bonfire rising into the sky. It's many spires topped by multi colored onion domes.

"That's St. Basil's," he said in a shaky voice.

"Yeah, we *are* in Red square you know."

"But, it-it's so beautiful."

"Yes, it can have that effect on people. Now keep moving."

Suddenly the crowd in front of them started to turn, like dominoes falling down. And a chill ran down Curial's spine as he became aware that the people were turning to stare.

At him.

"Oh no," he said.

Two men in suits slipped through the crowd, shouted in Russian and ran towards them.

Curial instinctively ran to the left side of the square,

Dina right behind him.

He was running for his life.

He was running to the GUM.

CHAPTER TWENTY

THE CHASE

Dina and Curial made it to the top of the steps at the same time, then opened the doors to the GUM and sprinted in.

As soon as he looked around, Curial was taken aback. To his left and right, shops lined three stories of a mall that seemed to extend forever in both directions. A glass domed ceiling covered the mall's entire length.

Dina raced to the right and headed up a flight of stairs. Curial followed her up to the second floor where she was walking quickly past two shops, then stopped and peaked over the railing. The same two men from Red Square came into the middle of the mall. To their right, more commotion as two men came running down the mall.

"My God," Curial said. "Where do all these guys keep coming from?"

"FSB, they're everywhere. Come on." Dina went into a luxury clothing shop and motioned for Curial to follow.

She walked to the side, then ducked behind a display of mannequins. Curial followed her. She was crouched low behind and he did the same.

"What are we doing?" asked Curial.

"It's called hiding, blockhead," Dina responded while peeking around the mannequin to look out into the store.

"I feel like a sitting duck."

"You feel like a duck?"

"It's an American saying, it means—"

"Shhhh!" Dina put her finger to her lips and pointed out into the store. One of the men had entered and was looking around.

Curial began to shake. Dina put a hand on his forearm and squeezed. He looked at her and she narrowed her eyes at him.

He waited for what seemed like an eternity, but it couldn't have been more than thirty seconds. Then the man started to walk back out of the store.

That's when the sneeze came. And it wasn't Curial. He turned to see Dina covering her mouth and then turned back to the store as the man re-entered and looked towards the mannequin display.

They were in trouble.

The man wasn't hesitating now. He was walking right towards them, a suspicious look on his face. Curial did the only thing he could think of. He grabbed the mannequin and, while screaming his head off, charged the man. Curial hit him full speed and the man toppled backwards. "Run, Dina, run!" Curial said as he scrambled to his feet. Dina hung a left out of the store and then screamed herself.

Curial ran out of the store to find one of the guys holding her, Dina kicking and clawing for her life. The man inside the store was on his feet now, coming right for Curial. He took a few steps toward Dina. "Get out of here Curial!" she yelled.

He hesitated. He heard angry Russian to his left and turned to see the man reaching for him.

Instinctively, like Hank had trained him to do countless times in the ring, Curial ducked, then he came up with a left followed by a right body blow. The man's chin dipped down just in time for Curial's left uppercut which hit the man flush on the chin, causing the man to shriek and stumble backwards while Curial felt like he'd just broken his hand against a brick wall.

He shook his hand as he looked back at Dina. He rushed towards her and when he did, she stomped on the foot of her attacker with the heel of her boot. The attacker let go and bent down just as Curial got there to deliver an overhand right that caught the guy in the jaw and sent him down to the marble corridor.

Dina looked at Curial with shock, her eyes wide with surprise. "You can fight?"

Curial shook his throbbing right hand. "I can box. Now let's go."

He and Dina sprinted past five more stores, took a walkway to the other side of the second floor corridor, then descended the stairs to the first floor, where she spotted another exit. They looked around. No scary men to be seen. They walked quickly out of the other side of the GUM, and Dina immediately started whistling for a cab. One stopped in the center of the street and Dina and Curial both jogged with their hands up.

A dark van came from their left and skidded to a stop in front of the cab. The door flew open. Arms grabbed Dina and Curial before they could run. Two men jumped out of the van and put dark bags over their heads.

Then as they kicked and screamed for their lives, Dina and Curial were carried into the van. Curial heard the door slide shut and the van surge forward, tires pealing in its wake.

Then he heard a strange click and felt something hard press up against his skull.

"Now please settle down," the voice said in heavily accented English. "I have a gun and I know how to use it."

CHAPTER TWENTY-ONE

KIDNAPPED

Being kidnapped in a strange country by men who had guns and knew how to use them was bad.

But Curial had been through worse.

When his mom was first diagnosed with cancer—that was bad. But then the treatment worked and she got better. And then one day, out of the blue, she changed. For the worse. The cancer was back, and this time nothing was stopping it. And she knew.

And Curial *knew* that she knew.

Caroline Diggs was going to die.

He cried himself to sleep that night. And the next night. And quite a few nights after that.

That was the most scared he'd ever been and as he sat, shrouded in darkness, feeling the vibrations of the van as it drove through Moscow, his thoughts stayed with his mother.

And then when the sound under the van changed from

mostly smooth concrete to crushed rock, the van suddenly stopped and the door opened. The man with the gun barked at him and Dina to move, and then Curial was dragged out of the van and dumped on the ground. He stumbled to his feet and someone pulled off his black hood.

Curial strained his eyes against the early evening rays of sun, peaking through the clouds in brilliant purples and pinks. He turned to see Dina looking at him, her breathing shallow, her eyes trying to communicate with him.

A man pushed him in the back of the shoulder and then they were walking. For the first time, Curial noticed he was in a driveway and looked to his left at the enormous neo-classical mansion. Mostly white, with yellow trim and green shutters. It looked, well, it looked like a museum.

The men walked him and Dina down the driveway, around the house and then through a back door. They walked up the steep steps of a narrow stairwell, up three flights. At the top of the stairs they turned right and walked down a narrow hallway with a ceiling dropped low and angled left to right, like they were walking through a funhouse. Then the man in front stopped in front of a yellow door and knocked three times. He pushed the door open and stood to the side. He waved Curial in.

Curial stepped in and was greeted by an older man. Sophisticated, powerful, dressed in a brown tailored suit. The man nodded.

"My name is Victor Koralenko, welcome to my home."

Then without waiting, Koralenko stepped to the side and Curial's eyes landed on Maurice. He was sitting in a chair, hands folded on the table in front of him. His eyes opened in surprise.

"I knew you'd find me! I told Victor here that we Americans don't leave men behind." Then Maurice's face suddenly hardened. "But don't tell this Russian pig a thing. I told him I wasn't going to rat out my best friend Curial Diggs. I told him it didn't matter what he did to me. Then he showed me a picture of an ancient Dutch torture device that appears to pull your arms out of their sockets, and I told him it might matter what he did to me...but thankfully it hasn't come to that yet."

"Shut-up Maurice," Curial said, then turned to Koralenko. Although Curial hadn't been kidnapped before, he was quite accustomed to being around and speaking with powerful and important people. He stood confidently. "I assume you know who I am?"

Koralenko tilted his head. "Naturally. The son of a very wealthy and very powerful man. It would be a shame to have to kill you. So just tell me why you and your friend have been asking about me and you can be on your way."

Maurice tried to stand up but a large Russian kept his hands on his shoulders. "Don't listen to him Curial, it's a trick. You can't trust these Rooskies, you've seen *Rocky 4* haven't you?"

Curial smiled at Koralenko. "You wouldn't kill me."

Koralenko shrugged and smiled back. "Look at you, smart poker player you are. You know I can't kill someone like you. Too important, too many questions. I confess, you got me."

Curial breathed a sigh of relief.

"Which means I'll just have to kill your friends." Koralenko waved with two fingers and two guards pulled Dina into the room.

"I said don't listen to him Curial, nothing but a trick."

But Curial wasn't so sure.

The Russian man holding Dina started squeezing her by the shoulders. Curial could see the strain in her face.

"Fine, I'll tell you."

"Don't do it!" Maurice yelled.

"We're looking for something, something valuable."

"Something with an old symbol on it?" Koralenko asked.

"Don't talk to this Russian pig Curial, don't do it!"

But Dina was silent, the large Russian continuing to squeeze, her face growing more and more red.

Koralenko waved his hand. "Because that's what my

sources in St. Petersburg told me. Said the mouthy one here was asking all about this symbol."

Curial nodded. "We're looking for…the Romanov Dolls."

Karalenko's face went rigid. He looked down at Maurice and then over at Dina. He nodded to the large Russian man and he instantly stopped squeezing Dina.

Then Koralenko began to laugh.

"I am a man who is not often surprised but I must admit, I wasn't expecting that." He pointed at Curial. "So you think I know where the Romanov Dolls are?"

"We know the symbol on the bottom of the dolls was put there by a group within the Russian secret police, one tasked with tracking down for Stalin objects with special powers. We know that your father ran that agency. We know that you, like your father, were KGB and we know that you are one of the foremost art collectors in Moscow."

"And that means I must have the Romanov Dolls."

"Don't you?" asked Curial.

Koralenko shook his head again, then licked his lips. "Look at you, rich American kid. So arrogant. So typical. You come into my country looking for a Russian treasure, one that nobody has found for forty years, and you think by talking to a woman at a museum you have figured it out."

"And have I?"

"Such a disappointment. I thought you kids might be spies. Believe it or not, your CIA and Israel's Mossad use young people sometimes. I was excited to try out some of the toys in the basement." Koralenko sighed. "But turns out, you're worse than spies, you're treasure hunters. And by the looks of it, very bad treasure hunters. I do not have the Romanov Dolls. They remain, as they've always been, a mystery. From their creation at Abramtsevo to their residence in Winter Palace to their traitorous voyage to America and then poof...not much has ever been understood about the Romanov Dolls. And if you must know, I wasn't even aware they had the symbol of my father's unit. You're sure about this?"

"I'm sure."

"Then I can only say the mystery continues." Koralenko looked at his watch. "And I'm afraid you kids are out of time."

Curial swallowed. "What do you mean?"

Dina stomped her foot. "My grandfather is a very important man in St. Petersburg, you can't do this to us."

Maurice strained forward. "I told you this Russian pig couldn't be trusted Curial."

Koralenko just shook his head in amusement. "Oh my, young people are always so dramatic. I'm not going to kill you. I haven't killed anyone in...well, it's been awhile.

Frankly, I'm out of practice. I meant you're making me late, I have a date to play bridge and I can't keep my partner waiting." He motioned with his fingers. "The boys will take you wherever you need to go."

Koralenko looked down at Maurice. "And if this one gives you trouble, just drag him from behind the van."

CHAPTER TWENTY-TWO

SERGIEV POSAD

Curial, Maurice, and Dina sat in the train station waiting for the SESPAN high speed train to arrive. Curial let out a long sigh. "Every single lead has resulted in a dead end. Every single lead."

"Of course," Maurice said overly loud, "I *am* alive and my arms are still attached to my body so there is that."

"I don't remember asking you to come to Russia to help me. Wait, in fact I remember expressly telling you not to come to Russia with me."

Maurice's expression soured. "You know what Curial, sometimes you're like the crappiest best friend I've ever had."

"I'm not your best friend, I'm not even your friend."

"Well you're sure not acting like my friend but..." Maurice raised a finger, "I of course *am* your friend so don't worry dude, if you and I have to take that private jet of yours around the globe, visiting the world's finest beaches and resorts to find those dolls, then that's just what we'll have to do."

"You're an idiot Maurice," Curial said.

"And you're a blockhead," reminded Dina. "So the two of you should be very happy together."

Curial stood up to stretch and found himself looking at the map of the trains. He was staring at the routes leading out of Moscow when a name jumped out at him.

"Abramtsevo Colony." He turned around.

"What did you say?" asked Dina.

"Abramtsevo, just northeast of Moscow."

Dina shrugged. "What about it?"

"Koralenko mentioned Abramtsevo. He said that's where the Romanov Dolls were created."

"You sure?" Maurice asked.

Curial nodded. "I'm sure."

Dina tapped on her knee. "Okay, so what?"

"My mom thought the symbol etched into the dolls was important because it might tell us something about who or how the dolls were created. Until now, we've had no luck finding out who made the dolls or where they were created."

Maurice smiled. "But apparently that good for nothing Rooskie Koralenko does."

Dina glared at Maurice. "You do realize you're surrounded by 140 million good for nothing Rooskies?"

"The guy threatened to pull my arms off, you want me to send him a Christmas Card?"

Curial interrupted. "And for some reason, Koralenko thinks the dolls were made in this place." He tapped on the map. "Abramtsevo. Wait a second, I know this name." Curial bent over and held his head, then looked back up, a smile on his face. He pointed at Dina. "When you and I were at the doll shop, I asked Valeeni if he thought it was possible that Vasily Zvyozdochkin (ZV-YOZ-DOACH-KEEN) might have carved the dolls. In my reading, I learned that he had carved the first Russian matryoshka dolls back in 1890 and was the most famous doll maker in Russia. I figured he would be the obvious person to make a special set of dolls for Czar Nicholas. But what I forgot until just now, is that Vasily made his dolls in?"

"Abramtsevo," Dina said, now standing up.

"Exactly."

Dina shook her head. "We've been so busy trying to find Maurice, I totally forgot."

"About what?"

"When we came out of Gennady and Valeeni's, Maurice found us right as I was trying to tell you."

"Time to tell me what?"

"Gennady, he was acting weird."

"What do you mean weird?"

"When you were asking him about how the Romanov Dolls were made, I think, well, I think he was lying to you."

"You think they know something about The Romanov Dolls?"

"I think Gennady knows something about how the dolls were made that he didn't want us to know."

"Which means we need to go to Abramtsevo. Is there a train going that way?"

"Not for an hour," said Maurice. Curial and Dina turned around. Maurice was twenty feet away, smiling. "But I think this bus might work."

Dina learned from the bus driver that just a few miles from Abramtsevo artist's colony was the town of Sergiev Posad, where the Abramtsevo Russian Toy Museum was housed. And so it was, that forty-five minutes after they left Moscow, the bus dropped them off in the heart of the village of Sergiev Posad. Dina asked directions and within a few minutes, they were walking up the steps of a steep hill, to a reddish brick building that was shaped like a long rectangle with a squared off castle turret covering the entrance doors.

Dina paid their admission, had another Russian conversation with an employee, and then walked confidently through the exhibits like she knew where she was going. And it didn't take Curial long to figure out what she wanted to show them.

The Matryoshka Doll exhibit.

And not just any matryoshka doll exhibit.

Dina pointed at the dolls behind a glass case. There were eight of them, the smaller four lined up in front of the larger four. All were exquisitely painted Russian peasant women.

"These were the very first Russian matryoshka dolls every made in 1890."

Maurice stepped closer. "These? Right here?"

Dina leaned in to read from the plaque next to the exhibit. "Made in 1890. Carved by Vasily Zvyozdochkin and painted by Sergiev Malytunin."

"They are really beautiful," said Curial.

"I bet they don't transform into a yellow sports car do they?" said Maurice.

Dina glared at him.

"But beautiful in their own way," Maurice said with a smile.

Dina laughed. "American boys are very strange." Then she walked over to a museum employee and asked him a question. Finally the employee started to speak in English and followed Dina back to the boys.

The man clapped his hands together and smiled. "I don't get many Americans to the museum. Tourists seem to prefer Moscow and Red Square. So, you want to know something about these Romanov Dolls?"

Curial shook his head. "No, we want to know something about *the* Romanov Dolls, you know, the ones made out of previous metals and fine jewels."

The employee's face filled with understanding. "Ahhh, *the* Romanov Dolls. I apologize but I'm not sure what I can tell you. In fact, as far as I know they were in America before they were stolen."

Curial leaned in. "But we were under the impression that the dolls might have been made here, in Abramtsevo?"

The man's brow furrowed and his lip curled up. "Well, I have never heard such a thing."

"So the famous Romanov Dolls were not made here?" said Dina.

The man shrugged. "I don't think anybody has any idea where they were made. It is a Russian toymaker mystery."

Curial practically growled. This was getting old fast.

"Well, the dolls were given to Alexei Romanov in 1909," said Curial. "Do you have any record of who was making dolls at Abramtsevo around that time?"

The man smiled. "Certainly."

"Really?" said Dina.

The man spun and motioned with his finger. He walked behind the matryoshka doll exhibit to a large leather bound book. He opened it carefully and started slowly moving the pages until he stopped and adjusted his glasses.

Then he turned. "Would you like to see?"

Dina squeezed next to the man with Curial and Maurice in behind. The man continued moving his finger back and forth across the page while speaking quickly in Russian. Then Dina's posture stiffened and she turned. "In 1909, Vasily Zvyozdochkin was still here at Abramtsevo, still making dolls," she said.

Curial made a face at Maurice. "It's as good a guess as any."

"Wait," the museum man said while holding his hand up palm out. "You kids think the great Vasily Zvyozdochkin made the Romanov Dolls?"

"And why not?" Curial answered. "He was the most famous doll maker in Russia and at the time the Romanov Dolls were made, he was still actively making dolls, plus he was here at Abramtsevo where we heard the dolls were made."

The man moved his finger and thumb around his chin. "And who told you the dolls were made here?"

"I'd rather not say," said Curial.

The man smirked. "Then it sounds to me like you are chasing after ghosts. You come to Abramtsevo chasing after ghosts, then you don't belong in the museum, you belong in the colony speaking to the old woman."

"The old woman?" asked Dina.

The man moved his hands up and down. "Yes, the crazy old woman over at the colony. She's been there forever, cleans the cottages, tells fairy tales. Sounds like she's the right person for the three of you. Now, if that's all, I have actual museum business to do. Good day."

CHAPTER TWENTY-THREE

THE OLD WOMAN

The three friends jogged from Sergiev Posad to the Artist's Colony and in less than ten minutes came to a small parking lot with a plaque announcing the artist's colony in Russian.

Beyond the parking lot was a crushed stone path which Curial followed. The path led them into the woods and then across a small wooden bridge that crossed a creek. On the other side of the creek, they spotted their first building, a wooden log cabin to their left. On the right was a small white farmhouse. As they followed the winding path, they spotted more buildings until Curial stopped and sniffed the air.

"Do you guys smell that?"

Maurice grimaced. "Oh yeah, sorry about that. Haven't been feeling the best."

"No Maurice, do you smell *that*!" Dina said while pointing to the distance, where smoke was steadily rising out of the chimney of a small cottage.

Dina led them to the cottage but before she could go up the small set of steps, the front door creaked open and a short old woman squeezed through. She wiped her hands on her apron then asked a question in Russian.

Dina responded.

The woman said something else and this time Dina's response was longer.

The woman suddenly looked to the east, in the direction of Sergiev Posad and shook her head, then she opened the door wide and invited them in.

"What'd you say to her?" Curial asked.

"I told her the museum man said she was a crazy old woman, but one look at her told me she had more sense than that guy ever would. So I told her we would love to visit and she invited us in for tea."

Curial and Maurice followed the two women into the small cottage. "Hey Curial, have you noticed we haven't eaten anything in a while?"

"Well, food is the least of my worries," said Curial.

"Really, because, I'm not sure how the rich live, but us poor common folk actually need food to survive."

The woman motioned for them to sit down, so Curial sat down in an old dusty recliner that faced a TV from the 1970's, the kind with the wood paneling and a huge pair of rabbit ear antennas. Dina sat in a rocking chair and

Maurice sat on the floor. "Don't worry about me guys. I don't need food and I don't need a chair."

The old woman was clanking around in the kitchen and Maurice lifted his nose into the air. "Do you guys smell *that*?" he asked.

"Seriously Maurice," Curial said. "This place is too small, you can't be doing that in here."

"No, Curial this is way better than a fart. This smells like food!"

Sure enough, the old woman returned from the kitchen with a loaf of bread on a plate. The bread was dark brown, with nuts, and steaming hot. She cut three thick slices, layered a slab of butter on each and then handed them out. And Curial noticed that Maurice received the largest piece.

They sat in virtual silence for the next few minutes as they chewed slowly on their bread. The best tasting, most delicious bread Curial had ever eaten. The woman smiled as they ate and when Maurice finally finished the last piece of his bread, he licked his thumb of all remaining residue and then gave a goofy grin. "Dina, would you mind telling her that I am officially in love."

Dina shrugged, then said something in Russian, and the woman smiled. Then she stood up and cut Maurice another slice of bread. Finally, Dina and the woman started to speak in Russian again.

Dina turned. "This woman's name is Mischa," Dina finally said. "She's the housekeeper for the cottages. Lives here alone. Has lived here for thirty years."

"Can you ask her if she knows anything about the creation of the Romanov Dolls?"

Dina shook her head. "Already asked. She didn't respond. She just smiled at me."

Curial sighed, and then Mischa said something else in Russian. She and Dina laughed and then finally the woman stared at Curial, as if she was studying him. Then finally, she stood and walked to a back room. She came back with what looked like an old photo album. She sat down next to Dina and opened it. The woman looked up with big eyes.

"She wants you both to come see," said Dina.

"Is there any chance she's got another loaf of bread hidden in that album?" Maurice asked hopefully.

The woman laughed as if she understood Maurice and then said something in Russia. "Um Maurice, she just said, 'get over here idiot' in Russian."

He smiled and stood up. "See, I'm growing on her."

The woman opened to a page with an old picture of a young woman sitting on a rocking chair on a porch with a baby in her lap. Dina translated the woman's Russian. "This is her baby boy Dmitry when he was only six months old."

She turned to another page, of a two or three year-old boy flying a kite with his mom. And then turned the page again of a young boy fishing. She kept turning the pages, and Curial and Maurice watched as an old woman showed them pictures from long ago, when she was a young woman raising her boy. Curial looked, and the old woman's eyes were wet.

She reached out her hand and grabbed Curial by the arm. She stared at him so intensely that it frightened him. Then she said something in Russian and once again, Dina translated.

"She says her Dmitry, he was a good boy. And she needs to know Curial, are you—are you a good boy?"

A chill ran down Curial's back and he shook the woman's arm away. He felt his breath caught in his throat. He shrugged.

"I don't know, I just don't know," he said.

Dina translated back to the woman and she folded her hands on top of her album and she smiled a wide warm smile. Then she looked up, nodded, and turned to the back of the album. To a picture so old, Curial could hardly believe it was a picture. Two Russian craftsman, one middle aged, one young, stood posing for the camera, shaking each other's hands. The joy from their smiles was contained by their wide bushy mustaches. The woman pointed to the words below the picture and Dina read.

"Vasily Zvyozdochkin and Ivan Belsky, 1909." Dina's eyes lit up and she smiled at Curial. But Curial noticed something about Mischa, she had a very different smile on her face. As if she was waiting for something.

And that's when Curial saw it. The old photo helped obscure the image, make it faded and almost ghostly, but there was no mistaking it. Behind the men, in the middle of them but behind so you could almost miss him, was another figure.

He was tall, owned wild eyes and crazy curly black hair. A scary figure. A figure all Russians knew, a figure most non-Russians even knew.

That's when Dina saw him too. She gasped and looked at Curial, whose heart was beating quickly.

"What's going on?" Maurice said while also staring at the picture.

"Then it's *really* him?" asked Curial.

Dina nodded. "Yes Curial, it is. That is without a doubt, Gregory Rasputin."

"I can't believe it," Curial said. "I just can't believe it."

Dina continued talking in Russian with the old woman who continued to rock back and forth, proudly holding her old picture album.

Curial stood up. "Dina, your grandfather, when I first met him, he said something to me. I told him I wanted to learn about the Romanovs and he said most people just want to know about Rasputin. I thought it was a joke. I can't believe Rasputin has something to do with this. What do you think it means?"

Dina's eyes were fixed on the picture, like she couldn't look away.

"Dina?"

She finally looked up, her finger stuck to the album like it couldn't move.

"I know," Curial said. "Rasputin. I didn't see that coming."

She shook her head. "No Curial, look closely."

He leaned over and noticed that her finger wasn't on Rasputin, nor on Vasily. It was on the other man, the younger man, the one called Ivan Belsky.

"Curial, who does this look like?"

He looked and then, as if all of a sudden, it hit him and the image made sense, like a puzzle that finally showed its true form.

"My God, that's—"

"Gennady," Dina said. "It looks like Gennady."

"But how is that even possible? The name here says Ivan Belsky and—"

"And Gennady's name is Lukin," Dina said. She stood up and handed the album back to the woman then said several things in Russian. Then she gave the woman a warm hug. The woman stepped over to Curial and gave him a warm hug as well. Then she turned to Maurice and gave him the longest and warmest hug. Then she handed him one more slice of bread and said something in Russian.

"I think I love that woman," Maurice said as he stepped outside.

But Curial almost didn't hear him. He was focused on Dina, who by now was already far away, jogging back towards Sergiev Posad. They followed her and ten minutes later they arrived back at the toy museum.

She went directly to the book, ignored the museum man, and opened back up to 1909.

"What's going on Dina, why did that picture look like Gennady?"

"I don't know, but I'm hoping this book will tell us." She ran her finger down the page. "Look here. Vasily Zvyozdochkin was working as a toy carver, and in 1907 he gained a new apprentice named Ivan Belsky.

Dina continued to drag her finger all the way down and then turned the page. "Looks like Zvyozdochkin made toys at Abramtsevo until 1913 at which point Belsky became a master but didn't take on an apprentice until..." She ran her finger down the page until she stopped. "Here, right here. His son Michael came to work for him as an apprentice in 1918 and then continued to work for him until he went off to the war." She started flipping pages. "There's a lot of names in here, and then the wars screw everything up...but...here, right here. In 1960, he took on a new apprentice." She looked up, her eyes dancing back and forth. "And his name was Gennady. Gennady Belsky."

"That seems like a very strange coincidence," offered Maurice.

Dina returned to the book and scanned furiously down the page until suddenly, she caught her breath. She held up one hand as if she'd just made some kind of discovery. "And in 1967, Gennady Belsky married a girl and her name was Valeeni Lukin."

Curial practically stumbled. "My God, so it really was them?"

But Dina continued to stare at the page. "And that's not all. It says here they left Abramtsevo in 1970. It doesn't say why, but they left."

"Wait a second," said Curial. "What year?"

"1970."

"That's the year the Romanov Dolls were stolen."

"Exactly."

"Dina, what's going on here? Is it typical to take the woman's last name in Russia?"

"Not at all."

"So Gennady Lukin, whose grandfather helped Vasily Zvyozdochkin make the Romanov Dolls—years later, he mysteriously takes the last name of the woman he marries, and then leaves for St. Petersburg the year those same Dolls were stolen?" Curial threw both hands in the air. "And somehow Rasputin, this crazy almost mythical figure in Russian History, is involved? Dina, what the heck does all of this mean?"

"Any chance it means we go back to the old woman's house and get more bread," said Maurice with a smile on his face.

Dina shook her head. "No Maurice, what it means is we've got to get back to St. Petersburg, and fast."

CHAPTER TWENTY-FOUR

BORIS MARKOFF

At the train station, all three kids were able to fill their bellies with something neither Curial nor Maurice could pronounce but was nonetheless delicious. And filling enough to help them each catch a nap on the four hour train ride back.

When they finally arrived back in St. Petersburg, they made their way directly to Dolls of Beauty. Curial and Maurice followed Dina through the door to the shop, and the little bell clinked against the window, just like Curial had remembered from the last time. Valeeni appeared from the hallway.

"We need to see Gennady," Dina said in a firm voice.

Valeeni halted, concern all over her face, then Dina walked right past her and Curial and Maurice followed.

They found Gennady working at his table, block of wood in one hand, carving knife in the other, white earbuds in his ears.

He smiled when he saw them, and lifted the earbuds out of his ears. Then he must have seen the expression on Dina's face because his mood seemed to instantly change.

"Dina? What is wrong?"

"When Curial and I were here asking you about the Romanov Dolls, you lied to us. You said you didn't know anything about how they were made."

He set the wood and carving knife down on his table. "What is this all about?"

"We just came from Abramtsevo, Gennady. Or should I say, Gennady Belsky."

Curial heard a small crash and turned to see Valeeni with her hands to her face, her tea cup smashed into pieces on the wood floor. Gennady seemed to stagger at the news and held a hand out to the table for support. Then slowly, he lowered himself into his chair.

Dina helped Valeeni into a chair next to Gennady. The old couple exchanged a long look, and then finally Valeeni reached for Gennady's hands and squeezed.

Gennady squeezed his wife's hands in reply, then let go and took off his glasses. He rubbed them and placed them back on the tip of his nose.

"I am an old man. All I've ever wanted to do is love this woman and make beautiful dolls. But I've lived under a cloud for far too long."

Dina leaned in. "What happened?"

"As you somehow discovered, I was raised with the name Gennady Belsky. My grandfather was Ivan Belsky, a great artist who worked alongside Vasily Zvyozdochkin (ZV-YOZ-DOACH-KEEN) at the crafts workshop at Abramtsevo."

Gennady paused a moment and looked over at Valeeni. She blinked back lovingly.

"Vasily is the one who gained all the fame. But my grandfather"—Gennady held his fist to his chest—"he was every bit the doll maker as Zvyozdochkin. And even though it is true that Vasily was commissioned to make the Romanov Dolls, my grandfather... he helped him."

"Seriously?" Curial leaned forward even more.

"My father was killed in the great war when I was a baby," Gennady continued, "and my mother and grandfather raised me. From a young age, I was taught by my grandfather how to make dolls, and when I was a teenager, I became his apprentice. And then, one day, when his hands didn't work as well and he was getting near the end, he told me." Gennady's eyes twinkled. "And what's more, he *showed* me."

Maurice exchanged a look with Curial. "Showed you what?"

Gennady took a long even breath through his nose, the kind that made his shoulders rise and fall, then turned to Valeeni and squeezed her hand again. He walked over to a wooden chest, opened it up, and pulled out a black metal cube.

Gennady took a deep breath. "A matryoshka doll is traditionally made of a single block of wood. It takes an extraordinary amount of skill to learn how to take a block of wood and, using nothing but a lathe, turn that into a nested doll with six, eight, or even twelve dolls.

"So when Czar Nicholas commissioned Vasily and my grandfather to make the dolls, they had a problem. The Czar didn't want a doll made of wood—he wanted one completely fashioned out of precious metals and jewels. Of course, Vasily and Ivan knew they could never make them in the traditional way. So they came up with a plan. They carved the dolls out of wood, and then made molds of those dolls."

Gennady unlatched the cube and pulled out what looked like a matryoshka doll—but it was made out of unpainted, dark brown clay.

"My grandfather told me that making these molds was painstaking work, yet he insisted they come out absolutely perfect. But finally, once the molds were ready, they started the process of melting down the gold and silver, and fashioning the dolls."

Curial pointed at the clay in Gennady's hands. "And these are the molds?"

"The very same."

Gennady laid the molds in the boy's hands, and Curial held them as if they themselves were a great treasure. He felt the weight of them, turned them over slowly in his hands. The Romanov Dolls, the treasure his mother had been obsessed with for her entire life, had been fashioned in *these* molds. These exact same molds. A chill ran down his spine. Finally he looked back to the old doll maker.

"There's something I don't get," Curial said. "And I mean no disrespect, but, well… using a mold to make the dolls hardly seems especially ingenious. Yet my mom talked about how the Romanov Dolls were so perfect that many people wondered how they were ever created. If it was really so simple, why were people so disbelieving?"

Gennady looked toward his wife again; she turned away and set her gaze into the corner of the room. At last Gennady spoke. "My grandfather said they worked for months and months on getting the dolls just right, and when they were finally finished, he and Vasily were very proud."

"But?"

"The day came for Vasily and Ivan to show off their work. The Czar was sending a representative to Abramtsevo to collect the work and pay their commission. But when the man arrived, it was no ordinary man…"

"It was Rasputin," Curial said.

Gennady's mouth fell open. "H-how did you—?"

"We saw a picture, we know Rasputin was there."

Gennady bit down on his lip, nodded, then continued. "Rasputin, even back then, even in the early years, he was known in Russia. There were rumors. That he was a holy man, some said a charlatan, some said a sorcerer. So when Rasputin came into the workshop to see their work, he took one glance at the dolls and…" Gennady couldn't find the right words, and asked Valeeni something in Russian.

She replied in English. "That madman lost his mind."

Gennady nodded. "That's it, Rasputin lost his mind. 'Not good enough for the royal family,' he told them. He was furious. Finally, he said he would have to fix things himself. He threw Vasily and Ivan out of their own workshop. My grandfather waited outside—outraged, but mostly humiliated. He felt like he had let the Czar down. He also felt like he had wasted months of his life on these dolls."

Gennady danced his fingers across his knee. "Fifteen torturous minutes later, the door opened, and Rasputin waved them back. As my grandfather walked in, he smelled something. He told me he would never ever forget that smell, like a cross between burnt hair and licorice, and the air was smoky. On the workshop table were the Romanov Dolls."

Gennady paused and looked up and into the corner of

the room. A smile spread across his face. Then he looked down at Curial. "And the dolls were perfect."

Curial felt like he'd just dropped down a roller coaster. "W-what do you mean?"

"They were the same dolls Vasily and my grandfather had fashioned, and yet, somehow, by someone or by something…they'd been made perfect." He shrugged. "Rasputin thanked the men for their work, paid them in full, and then he left. They never saw nor heard from him ever again."

The four of them sat in silence, Curial trying to process what it all meant. Maurice finally interrupted the silence.

"That is some seriously spooky stuff." Then Maurice leaned closer to Dina. "You think Valeeni here can bake as good as my old pal Mischa?"

Dina mouthed the words "Shut up" then turned her attention back to the old doll maker.

"Gennady," she said. "There's something I still don't understand. I get you not wanting to tell us about Rasputin. I do. But why did you need to change your name?"

Curial picked up on Dina's point. "And why did you move from Abramtsevo in 1970? I assume you know that's the same year the Romanov Dolls were stolen?"

Gennady nodded gravely. "When Ivan died, I carried on the family tradition and continued to make dolls at

Abramtsevo. I met Valeeni, and we got married and we had a nice life. It was a little life, but it was ours, and it was quite lovely. And we were happy."

Valeeni squeezed his knee. "We were *very* happy."

"A new artist came to the collective in the spring of 1969, by the name of Boris Markoff. He was young, had tremendous energy, was funny, charismatic, and I liked him immediately."

"But *I* didn't," Valeeni said as she rocked back in her chair.

"No, Valeeni thought Boris was too charming for his own good. Still, he and I became fast friends, and I taught him everything I knew about doll making. One night, after entirely too much vodka, Boris told me that in his previous life, he had been an accomplished thief. I told him I didn't want to know any more."

"Why?" Dina asked.

"Dina, Dina, Dina. You never grew up in Soviet Russia. There were eyes and ears everywhere. If Boris had done something wrong, I didn't want to know.

"Then another night, after *another* too many vodkas, I told Boris the story of the Romanov Dolls. He was incredibly interested and asked me a question. Did I think I could make dolls as good as the Romanov Dolls?"

"And you said yes," Maurice suggested.

"I said 'heck no!' Not a chance. I laughed it off and

didn't give it another thought."

"Until?" Curial asked.

Gennady sighed. "Four months later, Boris comes to me with a plan. Says he has a buyer who's willing to supply the precious metals and the gems if I would make a duplicate of the Romanov Dolls. I tell him it can't be done. He wants to know if I will try. I say I can't. Then he hands me more money than I've ever held in my life."

"And we should have given it back and said no." Valeeni rocked back again.

"But I didn't. I knew that with this money, Valeeni and I could follow our dreams. Our lovely little life wouldn't have to be so little after all. So I took the money. And I made the dolls."

"You made a set of Romanov Dolls?" Dina asked, her voice and body rising up at the same time.

"It took a lot of trial and error, even with the molds... but after much effort, I finally made something quite beautiful."

"But let me guess," Curial said. "Not perfect."

Gennady shook his head. "No, not perfect. At the time, Boris had been gone from the collective for a while. When he came back, he examined the dolls and said they would have to be good enough. Then he took the dolls and left."

Gennady paused.

"That's it?" Dina said.

"That was the last time we saw Boris. A month later, I was in my workshop, carving dolls, when Valeeni comes in, her face white as a ghost. She says the Romanov Dolls had been stolen from New York. Then a week later she came in, her face as white as a ghost again."

Valeeni stopped rocking.

"She heard in town from a friend of a friend. Boris was dead."

Dina cupped her hands to her face. "What happened?"

"I don't know, and Valeeni and I weren't going to stay around long enough to find out. I never had a good feeling about what I'd done. Money isn't free, especially that much money, and I had taken a shortcut and I knew it. I'd already endangered Valeeni enough with my stupidity and greed and I wasn't going to take any more chances. We left Abramtsevo the next day, moved to St. Petersburg, changed our names, and used the money to open our doll shop. And that was it."

"You really don't know how Boris died?" Curial asked.

"I don't even know where he died. I never *wanted* to know, but I had a pretty good idea what happened. I'm sure he had something to do with the theft of the Romanov Dolls and I'm guessing something went terribly wrong. But, like I said, in Soviet Russia, there were eyes and ears everywhere; if I had started poking around, getting interested in what happened to my friend, people would have been liable to take notice. So I just put my head down and tried to forget it happened."

Curial leaned back. "So when I show up out of the blue and start asking these questions…"

Gennady nodded. "It spooked us pretty good. Dina, we're sorry for lying."

"Does my grandfather know? Does he know who you really are?"

Gennady laughed. "Heavens no. Nobody knows except for the three of you. And Dina, if it's okay with you, we'd like to keep it that way."

Dina smiled. "I understand."

He looked at Maurice.

"Young man?"

"My silence can be purchased for the price of one small, delicious confectionary."

Dina punched him in the arm.

"Ow, fine I won't tell anybody."

"And Curial?" said Gennady.

Curial smiled. "Do you mind if I tell my friend Dina?"

Gennady laughed. "You're not bad for…"

Curial stood up. "For what?"

Gennady smiled and extended his hand. "For a blockheaded American."

CHAPTER TWENTY-FIVE

HOME INVASION

Curial and Maurice waited for Dina outside of the doll shop. When she finally came, she looked dazed. "I still can't believe it. I can't believe Gennady was wrapped up in all of this."

"You guys know what we have to do?" Curial said.

"What?" asked Dina.

"We have to find out who killed Boris Markoff."

"Curial's right," Maurice said. "We find out who killed Markoff, and I bet we'll solve this mystery once and for all."

Dina tapped her foot. "Okay, best chance we've got are the newspapers from back then."

"1970?" Maurice said. "Where we gonna find newspapers from 1970?"

"You're kidding me," said Dina, "Haven't you done a research paper before?"

Maurice shrugged. "Is this a trick question?"

"The library," Curial said. "The library has newspapers right?"

"Right," said Dina, "but with Grandfather's party tonight, I don't have time to go to the library."

"Wait, you've got a party to go to?" asked Curial.

"Yeah, well, my mother sent me a few texts reminding me that my attendance was required at one of Grandfather's parties."

Dina suddenly smiled and pointed at Curial. "You know what, you should come. Those parties are boring and full of nothing but old people."

Curial sighed. "You have no idea how many parties with boring old people I've had to attend in my life."

Dina glared at him. "Then one more won't kill you. Maurice, you up for it?"

"Will there be food at this party?" asked Maurice.

"Yep," said Dina.

"Then I am most definitely up for a party."

"But back to Markov," said Curial. "If you don't have time for the library, how do we figure out who killed him?"

Dina held up her phone. "Luckily, being the granddaughter of a university professor has it's privileges. I have a code that allows me to access all the digital microfilm of the college's old newspapers."

She pulled up an app and then started typing. She

clicked the tab for English so Curial and Maurice could follow along and then typed "Boris Markoff" into the query field. After a few seconds the results showed up.

"Russia is a very large country," she said. "And there are apparently a *lot* of Boris Markoffs. Too many. We need to narrow the search parameters." Dina typed "death 1970" in the search field and hit enter again.

This time a few more seconds passed, and then only a handful of results came up. Curial scanned the entries and saw one that was a newspaper article. Dina clicked on the "translate" button and then the article came up in English.

Burglar Shot In Home Invasion

Dina and Curial were almost cheek to cheek as they scanned the article together. Finally, Curial's eyes landed on one passage:

A man identified as Boris Markoff was shot in St. Petersburg early Saturday morning while trying to break in to the home of a prominent St. Petersburg figure. Authorities have not released any more details of the shooting other than to confirm the incident took place at the White Hills Estate of Anton Koralenko.

Curial's heart stopped when he saw that name.

"Oh my God," Dina said as she grabbed Curial's forearm and squeezed. Maurice pushed in between them.

"Anton Koralenko!" Maurice howled. "I knew it, I

knew those dirty no good Koralenkos were behind this the whole time. You don't threaten to pull a kid's limbs off unless you're pretty messed up. I'll remind you that I had figured out Koralenko was behind this after just a few hours."

Curial shook his head. "I guess you were right."

"So what do we do?" asked Dina.

Curial swallowed. The *truth*. He finally knew the truth. Part of him figured that he'd probably never actually figure it out. But now that he did?

He swallowed again. Dina and Maurice were both looking at him, waiting on him.

"In less than forty-eight hours, one of my mom's oldest and dearest friends is going to lose the only job he's ever known unless I can bring home the Romanov Dolls."

"So what are you saying Curial?" said Dina.

"I'm saying tonight is my last chance to get them back."

Dina frowned. "But my grandfather's party is tonight."

"I know. Maurice, if you did some poking around with your street contacts, do you think you could figure out where a guy like Koralenko might hide something as valuable as the Romanov Dolls?"

Maurice curled up his lip. "No problem. And if I do figure it out, what then boss?"

Curial licked his lips, took a big sigh so that his

shoulders rose and fell. "Then I guess…w-we have to get them."

Maurice smiled and clapped his hands together. "Now that's what I'm talking about."

Dina's eyes grew big. "We're going to steal the Romanov Dolls from Victor Koralenko?"

"No Dina, this isn't your fight. The less you're involved from here on out the better."

Dina punched Curial in the shoulder.

"Ouch!" said Curial. "You know, at some point my shoulders are going to stop functioning because of you."

"Don't do that," said Dina, her jaw set tight.

"Don't do what?" Curial answered.

"You should have saved your little speech for *before* I was kidnapped outside of Red Square. No, after everything you've already put me through—there is no way I'm backing out of this now."

"You're sure?"

Dina folded her arms across her chest and stood tall. "I'm sure."

"Okay then, Maurice, can you plan a job this fast?"

Maurice bit his lower lip. "Maybe."

"We'll need better than maybe," said Curial.

Maurice smiled. "Well then maybe you better not every ask me a question like that again because of course I can!"

"Okay then. Maurice, when you've got everything ready, you come to the party and go over the plan with Dina and I."

"And then?" asked Dina.

"And then," said Curial, "we go get those dolls."

CHAPTER TWENTY-SIX

THE PARTY

Two hours later, Mike drove Curial through an enormous black wrought-iron gate then down a long blacktop drive, old-fashioned lamps lighting the way. He turned into a circular drive. Curial looked out with astonishment at the enormity of the house and the gathering.

Professor Ardankin was apparently rich. *Very rich*, Curial thought. Funny that Dina never mentioned it.

Curial followed a group entering the house and then began moving through the crowd. As he took in the opulence of the grand home, he couldn't help but notice that people kept staring at him. But after a lifetime of people staring, he had become used to it.

He squeezed through the crowd and made it to the edge of the great ballroom. The house was old and full of art—spectacular art. By the looks of it, Professor Ardankin's house could also double as an art museum.

Just how a college teacher made this kind of money, Curial couldn't quite figure.

Curial took the main stairwell up to the second floor. A large security guard looked at him strangely but Curial walked past without a word. The second floor was full of statues—not Italian-renaissance quality, but beautiful nonetheless. Professor Ardankin apparently had a keen eye for quality.

"Are you lost?"

Curial jumped, then spun and saw Dina ten feet away. At least, he thought it was Dina. This girl was dressed in a long silver gown, had her hair up, wore makeup, and definitely didn't look thirteen.

"What have you done with Dina Ardankin, the profoundly mean Russian girl who's been guiding me around Russia the past two days?"

She narrowed her eyes. "Shut it."

Curial stepped closer and put his finger to his chin. "You know, you look very…"

Dina glared at him. "My grandfather makes me dress fancy for these parties."

"But like I said, you look—"

She held her finger up. "Not a word." She looked around. "So what do you think?"

"It's not every day I get to visit a big Russian house. Funny how with all your rich American jokes you conveniently forgot to mention that you were also rich."

"I'm not rich," she said. "My grandfather is."

Curial smiled. "You know, I should really use that line. How about giving me a tour of this modest home?"

Downstairs, music started up and Dina's expression changed. "Listen, Grandfather expects me to dance certain dances during the evening and normally I have to do it with smelly old guys."

"Your point?"

She smiled and grabbed his hand. "Not tonight. Tonight I dance with you."

Dina dragged Curial down the stairs and before he knew it, he was on the dance floor. His palms were sweaty, his feet were clumsy, and he was twirling around the floor with an impossibly beautiful Russian girl who had helped him figure out more about the Romanov Dolls than anybody else had learned for forty years. He sure hoped his mother was watching him now.

Curial and Dina danced through three songs before a commotion at the front door caused them to stop. They turned to see Maurice trying to get in the party while a large Russian security guard held him by his collar.

"Oh the brutality!" Maurice cried when he saw Dina and Curial. "You tell this goon that unless he wants a rug burn on his hand from strangling me to death, he better let me go."

Dina laughed and then addressed the man in Russian. He promptly let go and Maurice collapsed in a heap onto the marble floor. He stood up, collected a black backpack and looked around. "Nice joint Dina, how exactly does a History Professor get a house like this?"

"I was sort of wondering the same thing myself," Curial said as Dina shook her head.

"He told me he inherited it from his father, that's all I know," she said. Then she pointed at the backpack. "Does that mean you've got a plan?"

Maurice smiled. "Was there ever any doubt?"

Dina led the way through the crowd until she came to a back room. She opened the door and led them to a round table. "Okay then, what have you got?"

Maurice unzipped his backpack and pulled out a set of plans and a series of photographs. He spread them out on the table. "Okay, you know how Koralenko's Moscow house was like a museum? Well, his St. Petersburg house, White Hills—it actually is a museum."

"What are you talking about?" asked Dina.

"Four nights a week, the first floor of his house is open as a museum. And guess what, we just got very unlucky. Tonight, the museum is open."

"Why is that unlucky?" asked Curial.

"More people, more eyeballs. It will be a lot easier for somebody to see you climbing up to the third floor window."

Curial's mouth went dry. "What do you mean 'climbing up to the third floor window?'"

"Right here," Maurice pointed. "You told me to figure out if Koralenko has the type of room where someone might keep something as valuable as The Romanov Dolls? Well, my contact says yes. On the third floor, there is a secure room and he has it on good authority it's protected by an electronic lock with a digital keypad. Told me it was state of the art."

"And you don't know how to bypass it?" asked Dina.

Maurice recoiled. "Of course I do. That's not the biggest problem. If Koralenko's got a room like that on the third floor, Lord only knows what kind of security he has leading up to it. Which means the easiest way to get through those layers of security is to avoid them. And that means climbing to the third story."

Maurice tapped on a photo of the side of the old stone house, a forty foot vertical face. Curial felt the panic already. He stepped back, his hands shaking.

"I-I can't climb."

"Sure you can," said Maurice. "I've even got some cool new gadgets to help you out."

Curial shook his head. "You don't understand, I can't do that."

Maurice exchanged a worried look with Dina and then turned back to Curial. "This path has the least chance for error."

Curial bit down on his fingernails. "Wouldn't falling to my death be an error?"

"From that height? Death isn't likely. Nope, from that height you're much more likely to break your spine, crush your bones, that kind of thing."

"Not helping," said Curial.

Maurice made a face. "You wouldn't be dead, but you might be sipping food through a straw the rest of your life."

Curial gritted his teeth. "I said not helping! Maurice, I'm not climbing, there's got to be another way."

Maurice looked at Curial then over at Dina and back. Then he studied the building plan and the photos. He took a breath. "Well, I guess we use Dina as a decoy."

"Meaning what?" Curial asked.

"Well, she goes into the museum, she looks around for security measures, when she finds a good window on the first floor, she lets you in and then together you make your way up to the third floor." Maurice scratched his chin. "But I'll need to walk you through every step of the way and you'll probably encounter several people, like humans; humans who have guns and know how to use them…and you'll have to get past them."

Curial sighed. "But with you talking us through it, you think we can do it?

Maurice leaned over the map and took another look.

"Probably. But like I said, there's an easier way."

Dina shook her head. "Move on Maurice."

Maurice hesitated a moment, then returned his eyes to the map and jabbed his finger at one of the pictures. "Okay, there is one guard at the gate. He's lazy and likes to read. All he's good for is keeping drivers away. The real security on the grounds is a hound dog named Vladimir." Maurice reached into his bag and pulled out a white bone. "We throw this over the fence and wait five minutes."

Curial took it. "A bone?"

"Trust me. It's coated in a secret ingredient. It won't hurt the dog—just give him a nice long nap."

"Dina, after you locate the correct window for Curial to come through, we'll still have to deactivate whatever security measures it might have." Maurice pulled out a close-up picture of one of the east windows. "Near as I can tell, it's a simple Denoyev Switch."

"And that's good?" asked Dina.

Maurice shook his head. "That's bad. Simple is usually bad."

Maurice pulled out a small device that looked like a battery charger and handed it to Curial. "It's called a Microburst. You attach this to the window here." He pointed to the underside. "Then you turn it on like this. Three seconds later, it radiates an intense electromagnetic pulse. It will knock out the alarm for long enough to get inside."

"But that sounds really easy," said Curial.

Maurice laughed. "Only works two out of five times."

"And what are my chances?"

Maurice made a weird face. "Let's move on, okay? Now should you cross the yard without being mauled by Vladmir, and should you enter the house without setting off the alarms, and should you somehow manage to avoid security until you get to the secure room on the third floor, there is still the matter of the electronic lock protecting that room." He pulled out a photo. "My contact said the lock and keypad are sophisticated—top of the line. Dealing with it appropriately is expensive."

Curial shook his head. "Expensive's not a problem."

"That's what I told my contact."

Maurice took a square, silver device out of his bag. "You will set this device over the keypad and attach this red wire to the port in the keypad. The decryption program will take thirty seconds or so, but it will give us the most commonly used keystrokes used over the past month to help us figure out the four or five digit pass code."

"It can't give me the exact code?" said Curial.

"Listen, this isn't like the movies. Like I said, Koralenko's system is sophisticated, and this is the best we can do. I'll be at a laptop not far from you, in communication the entire time through this ear piece."

Maurice handed Curial a small transmitter. "Once we come up with the most common letters, then I can help you figure the code out."

"But what if we can't figure out the code?" asked Curial.

"You got this far didn't you?" said Maurice.

"What's that supposed to mean?" asked Curial.

Dina shoved him. "It means that even for a blockhead, you're pretty smart."

Maurice raised his finger like he'd forgotten something. "And if you can't guess the code within three tries, the system will reboot and you'll have no chance of getting that door open."

Curial let that information sink in. "Is that it?" he asked.

Maurice shook his head. "Only this. My contact said the Koralenko is about as ruthless as they come."

"What are you saying?"

"I'm saying—are you sure you want to go through with this?"

Curial thought about it for a moment and then finally, nodded. "Viktor Koralenko took something from my mom. And I want it back."

Maurice smiled. "Okay then, how soon can we get started?"

Both boys looked to Dina. She growled.

"Unfortunately, grandfather will expect me to stay for the grand dance. I leave before then, and I'll have problems."

"Okay," said Maurice. "I'll go wait outside, find a bush, and go over everything from my end. And you two love birds can spend the rest of the evening twirling about on the dance floor."

Dina turned to Curial. "Am I allowed to kill him now?"

Curial smiled. "I'd prefer you wait until after we get those dolls back."

Dina's face fell in disappointment. "Fine. I've had enough dancing for a while. It's time to give you that tour."

CHAPTER TWENTY-SEVEN

THE ART COLLECTOR

Just as she'd been for the two previous days, Dina was the ultimate tour guide, telling Curial the history behind every piece of art, every room, and every spot in her grandfather's house that was special to her for one reason or another. Where she used to play hide-and-seek, where she broke her arm, where she practiced ballet as a little girl.

The third floor was more of the same—until they made their way to the farthest corner, where a large, hand-carved wooden door stood.

"What's in *there*?" Curial asked.

Dina's face went still. "That's nothing."

"Can I see it?"

Dina looked at the door, then looked at Curial and shook her head. "It was my Uncle Nikolai's room. He was my grandfather's only son, my mom's older brother. He died when he was, I don't know, six or seven years old."

"Wow, I'm sorry."

"My mom barely knew him but the hemophilia was such a terrible disease—well, I guess the whole thing was so hard on grandfather that he locked Nikolai's room and has never let anybody in there in years."

"Wait a second," said Curial. "Your uncle had hemophilia just like Alexei Romanov?"

"Yeah, I already told you I had a relative who had hemophilia, that's how I knew about the disease." Dina nodded her head the other direction. "Come on, I hear grandfather giving his speech. That means the grand dance is just a few minutes away."

Dina took off, leaving Curial behind as was her custom. But Curial was staring at the door to her uncle's room. The door wasn't just locked. It had an electronic keypad. Similar to the one in the picture Maurice has shown him of the kind of lock they would find in Koralenko's house.

"Curial, you coming or not?"

Dina was waiting impatiently at the top of the stairs next to a rather scary looking security man. Curial followed her all the way down to the first floor where there was a rush of excitement at the door as someone new had arrived.

And from the looks of the reception, this someone new was important.

Professor Ardankin smiled at Dina and Curial as he walked past them towards the front door and as Dina held out her hand for Curial to take it and go to the dance floor. That's when Curial heard Ardankin's professorial voice.

"Victor, what a surprise for you to make it, I thought you'd be in Moscow."

Victor? Curial spun around to see Professor Ardankin embracing another man around his age. A crowd formed around them and Curial instinctively moved their way.

"Curial, what is it?" asked Dina, but he ignored her. He walked towards Ardankin until finally the old professor moved to the side enough for Curial to see who this very important Victor was.

Curial froze. It was Victor Koralenko.

Koralenko saw him immediately and gave him a mysterious look. "Why Valery, won't you please introduce me to your American guest?"

Ardankin turned and seemed surprised to have Curial standing so near him. "Ahh yes Victor, you of course know of the great Robert Diggs, head of the Diggs Bank...well this is none other than his son...Curial."

"Extraordinary," Koralenko said as he waved his hand in a kind of salute. "Victor Koralenko young man. What a privilege to meet you."

Ardankin looked past Curial. "And this Victor, is the jewel of my collection, my granddaughter, Dina."

Dina exchanged a shocked look with Curial and then held out her hand to receive Koralenko's. She was stunned.

"H-how do the two you of you know one another?" Curial finally asked.

"A long boring story," Professor Ardankin said.

"Only when you tell it Valery," Koralenko said as he wrapped an arm around Ardankin and squeezed. "Truth is, we knew each other when we were young. You could say I made Valery what he is today."

Ardankin rolled his eyes. "I'd like to think I had a little something to do with my own success."

Koralenko chortled. "Very little but face facts. It was my father who gave you your start, did he not?"

Dina stepped forward. "What do you mean?"

"I mean that when your grandfather was a young man, he had an advanced degree in art history and little else. And my father gave him his start."

"You worked for him?" asked Curial while looking from Ardankin to Koralenko.

"Victor likes to *think* I worked for him," said the Professor. "I worked for his father, managing his private art collection at his White Hills estate. I worked there for only a few short years."

Koralenko beamed. "Before he used his own extraordinary brilliance to build this great legacy. Valery is right on that account. Okay, enough of the chit chat. I want your best vodka and I want it now." Koralenko gave one more mysterious look to Dina and then Curial. "It was a pleasure meeting you both."

And with that, Koralenko was off, Professor Ardankin was at his side, and Curial was left trying to process what it all meant.

"Did you have any idea your grandfather worked for Victor Koralenko?"

Dina was tapping her foot. "I think I would have mentioned that to you."

"Doesn't that seem weird to you?"

"Yeah, it does but, then again, St. Petersburg might be big…but not so big when you're rich. I guess it makes sense that my grandfather knows Koralenko." The orchestra music started up. "Listen, the easiest way for me to get out of here is to get the grand dance out of the way. And I'd rather do it with you than a bunch of smelly old guys. Come on."

Curial hesitated, then followed her onto the floor. "Dina, why again do they call this the grand dance?"

"Because it lasts an hour."

"Excuse me?"

She grabbed his hands. "You heard me, an hour. Now

let's get this over with."

"You do realize that hurrying won't actually make time go faster right?"

Dina narrowed her eyes. "Would you just shut up and dance?" And so they did. Dina and Curial danced. They spun around the room, he occasionally stepped on her feet, but for the most part they got around okay. Unfortunately, he had a hard time focusing on the beautiful girl in front of him.

Instead, all he could think about was that bedroom. Nikolai's room. A room that nobody entered. Curial understood the grief that came from losing someone you loved. He understood wanting to keep the memory of that person intact. But the fact that Professor Ardankin had a son with hemophilia just like Alexei Romanov? The coincidence was eerie. *Too* eerie for Curial. And then there was that lock, the boy's old bedroom was protected by an electronic lock. And from the looks of it, a sophisticated electronic lock.

But what, if anything, did it all mean? If Gennady was telling the truth, then it was Rasputin—through some sort of power or sorcery—who had elevated the Romanov Dolls from merely beautiful to unspeakably perfect. But what on earth would all of that have to do with a Russian History Professor?

He stopped and stepped away from Dina.

"What's wrong?" she asked.

"I need to use the restroom."

She gave him a weird look. "Oh, okay. Sure. I'll go get some punch but don't take too long. When grandfather says he expects me to do the grand dance he means *all* of the grand dance."

Curial gave a slight bow. "Then I'll be quick."

Curial turned and walked quickly in the direction of the restrooms. Along the way, he grabbed the small transmitter from his front pocket, turned the tiny switch on, and stuck it in his right ear.

"Can you hear me Maurice?"

"Dude, you guys about ready? I'm getting a little creeped out hanging in these bushes all by myself."

"Not quite but I need your help first. Something's not making sense. I need you to go online and check out Rasputin. I'd heard stories about him being a Holy man or a sorcerer. Try to find a connection between him and Alexei Romanov."

"What exactly does this have to do with my plan?" asked Maurice.

"Just do a search, okay?"

"Fine, fine. I'm just the kid who broke this case open from the beginning. No need to keep me in the loop. Whatever. Okay, bringing up results right now. Okay...got something. In fact, the next three results all talk about the same thing."

"And Maurice, would you mind sharing it with me?"

"You rich kids don't have very good manners do you?"

"Would you please share it with me?"

"Better," said Maurice. "According to this, people thought Rasputin had a special connection to the power of God and was capable of healing. Says here that he might have been responsible for healing Alexei's hemophilia."

It hit Curial like a freight train. "Oh my God. That's it!"

"That's what?" asked Maurice.

"Maurice, I know this is going to sound crazy but what if I told you I thought it was Professor Ardankin who actually stole the Romanov Dolls?"

"What?" squeaked Maurice.

"Just listen," said Curial. "Dina showed me a room tonight, nobody ever goes in it, and it's protected by the same kind of electronic lock you showed me in those pictures."

"Ha, that's all you got? Curial, this Ardankin's a rich dude. Not too surprising that he would have a special room for special stuff, if you know what I mean."

"No it's not surprising," said Curial, "but get this. This room apparently belonged to Dina's uncle. He died when he was a young boy. And check this out, he died...of hemophilia."

"You're kidding me?" said Maurice.

"I am not," said Curial. "What if? Well, what if Ardankin somehow figured it out. He figured out that Rasputin helped create the dolls, that the dolls had some special power, and that this special power had helped heal Alexei Romanov of his hemophilia."

"Wow, Curial, that's messed up. But it doesn't make sense. You told me yourself. The guy who killed Markoff is the one who stole the Romanov Dolls. And that's Victor Koralenko."

Curial shook his head. "No, that's just it. The killing took place at Koralenkos but the newspaper never identified the shooter as Koralenko himself."

"I just think you're grasping at straws," said Maurice. "You're saying that Ardankin would have had to coincidentally been at White Hills the day Boris Markoff was there."

"No Maurice, you don't understand. Koralenko is at the party tonight."

"Right now!" yelled Maurice.

"Yes, right now," said Curial. "Turns out he and Ardankin are old friends. Koralenko said Ardankin used to work at White Hills when he was a young man."

"He used to work there?"

"Do another search. Search Valery Ardankin, biography. Try to find some mention of him working for Koralenko."

"Got it. Okay, translating the page. Da, da, dah. Nothing on this one. Here's one from a speech he gave a year ago."

"Hurry Maurice," said Curial.

"Um, okay, early life, career…well what do you know? Says here that Ardankin started out as an art collector at none other than White Hills, the Koralenko estate."

"Years, Maurice, what years…"

"Okay, um got it, he worked there from 1968 to 1971. Wait a second Curial, he worked there…"

Dina was walking towards Curial now.

"When Koralenko killed Boris Markov," said Maurice.

"No Maurice, I don't think you understand. It wasn't Koralenko at all. It was Ardankin. Professor Ardankin was the one who killed Boris Markov."

"Are you crazy?" said Maurice.

"No Maurice, It *was* Ardankin. I'm sure of it. Valery Ardankin stole the Romanov Dolls," said Curial.

"You're serious?"

Curial watched as Dina got closer. "Unfortunately, yes Maurice, I'm serious."

"And I don't suppose you have any grand theory of where those dolls might now be?"

Curial thought of Nikolai's bedroom, the one nobody ever went into. The one with the electronic lock and he looked up at the ceiling. "If I'm right? About forty feet above my head."

"Dude! Dina is going to completely flip when you tell her."

She was almost too him now.

"I know, which is exactly why I'm not going to tell her," said Curial, turning his head so Dina couldn't see him talking.

"Then what are you going to do?" asked Maurice.

"The only thing I can do," said Curial. "I have to get rid of her."

CHAPTER TWENTY-EIGHT

OR NOT TO CLIMB

"You talking to Maurice?" asked Dina as she motioned to Curial's earpiece.

"Yeah, just got done telling him Koralenko was here. Pretty creepy don't you think?"

"Definitely creepy. And to think Grandfather knows him."

"He's known him for a long time," said Curial.

Dina hesitated. "It makes me wonder."

"About?"

"You think there's any chance my grandfather knows what Koralenko did?"

Curial studied her. Dina's eyes were dancing, like she was trying to figure something out, but nothing had come to her yet.

"Probably not," said Curial. "But we don't have time to think about that now. Maurice thinks that with Koralenko here at the party, it's probably our best chance to go."

"But the grand dance isn't finished yet."

"Yeah, about that. Maurice and I agree that Koralenko might get suspicious if you and I walk out together. Maurice and I will go to Koralenko's now, scout the place out and set up, and then you should follow when the grand dance is finished."

She gave him an odd look. "Really?"

"You know, just to be safe," Curial said.

"So you're going to make me dance the rest of the grand dance with a smelly old guy."

"Dina, I've only got one shot at getting those dolls back. You can handle a smelly guy for ten minutes."

"I suppose," she said. "I have been hanging out with you for the last few days, right?"

"Well played Dina Ardankin, well played."

She grinned. "Get out of here blockhead. I'll meet up with you soon."

Curial watched Dina walk towards a group speaking with her grandfather then he left the party. He walked out the front gate, took a left, looked behind him to make sure no one was following, then stepped off the sidewalk and lost himself in the trees. A hundred feet later, he came to the corner of the eight-foot wrought iron fence that bordered Ardankin's estate.

He looked down at Maurice who was dressed from head to toe in black, and sat on the ground with a computer perched on his lap and headphones covering his ears. He lifted one of them up.

"She went for it," Curial said.

"I heard. You really think this is a good idea not telling her?"

"It would break her heart if she knew the truth about her grandfather."

"So instead, you're just going to steal a priceless treasure from underneath her grandfather's nose and then leave Russia without ever telling her?"

"I really hadn't thought it out like that."

"Well, I'm just proud you decided to get over your fear and do the climb."

Curial froze. "What are you talking about Maurice?"

"Oh, my bad. So you're going to go back into the party and go up to the third floor room all by yourself?"

Curial kicked the ground. "There's no way I can get past the security guards without Dina."

Maurice danced his tongue along his bottom lip, then looked through the wrought iron fence at the Ardankin house. Then he looked back at Curial.

"Then like I said, that leaves only one way right?"

"I have to climb?" said Curial, his voice shaking.

"You have to climb," said Maurice.

"But I-I..."

Maurice nodded as if he understood, then he unzipped

his bag and pulled out black gloves and black slippers. They were shiny, like the kind of material scuba divers might wear. "Listen, my contact gave me these, said they are top of the line. They provide extra stick."

"Like Spiderman?" asked Curial.

"Not quite," said Maurice. "You've got to do the climbing on your own, but these will help."

Curial studied the distance from the ground to the third floor of Ardankin's house. It might as well have been a mountain to him.

"You mind telling me why the climbing thing has you so spooked?" asked Maurice.

"Yeah, I would mind."

Maurice opened up his arms. "Then maybe we should just hug it out?"

"Don't touch me," growled Curial.

Maurice grinned. "I've been told my hugs are therapeutic."

"No chance you know what the word therapeutic means," said Curial.

"It would be a shame to let a little thing like fear keep you from fulfilling your mother's dying wishes."

"Watch it."

"I'm just saying, a little fear or a priceless treasure?"

Curial put his head down and tried to control his breathing. After what seemed like an eternity, he finally looked up, grabbed the bars of the wrought iron fence and squeezed.

"How do I get past the dog again?"

"Now you're talking," said Maurice. "Better suit up."

Curial shook his head, and took off his tuxedo. Underneath, he had a long black jumpsuit. He finished by putting a black stocking cap on, then made sure the earpiece was still nice and snug. He slid a small black backpack through his arms.

Maurice held out the special dog bone and pointed to the lawn. A large grey German Shepherd lay near the corner of the house where the front yard merged into the side yard. The dog's eyes were open, his tongue out. Maurice flipped on a tiny switch at the base of the bone, then handed it to Curial.

"I'm guessing you got a better arm than me," said Maurice. "Now remember, if he doesn't take the bone, then you'll have to outrun that dog to the house."

"I can't outrun a dog."

Maurice slapped Curial on the back. "Then I guess he better take the bone."

Among other things, this special bone made a high-frequency sound that had been designed to attract dogs. Curial chucked it over the fence and watched as it landed in the grass about twenty yards away. The dog rose off his belly, barked, and ran to it. He spent a few moments sniffing it before he took his first lick. Then another. Then he sank his teeth in and started going nuts. If Maurice was right, the dog was now licking up the "secret ingredient" and would be getting sleepy soon. Curial checked the time on his phone and watched the dog. He spotted the window he would need to get to, then looked back at the dog again.

In three minutes, the big German Shepherd was sound asleep in the middle of the yard. Curial took a deep breath.

"You got this dude," Maurice said as he patted him on the back once more.

Curial wasn't so sure. Not at all. He scanned left and right, then climbed over the wrought iron fence and dropped to the other side. He crouched low, scanned back and forth again and sprinted across the lawn.

When he reached the house, he stood with his back pushed up against the wall and tried to catch his breath— but his heart was beating furiously, and his breaths were quick and shallow. Curial bent down, hands on his knees. He was feeling dizzy. *Keep—it—together*, he told himself.

When he was calm enough to continue, Curial moved down the east side of the house until he came to the spot he was looking for. He carefully inched his head past the edge of a first floor window and peered in. The party was winding down, with people beginning to leave. He sure hoped Dina was gone by now.

Curial crawled along the house until he made it to the third column of windows. He looked up at the third-floor window and swallowed hard.

From a distance, tall things always looked tall enough. But up close? To Curial, that third story window might as well have been the top of the Eiffel Tower. He started to shake and he pressed his hands against the stone on the side of the house and pressed hard. He turned around and scanned the lawn. The big dog was sleeping and beyond him, the wrought iron fence and the trees and Maurice. Curial could leave. He could leave right now. Get on that plane tomorrow and go back to New York like nothing happened.

He *could* do that.

His mom would forgive him. She loved him, she was his mom.

That was it, of course. Caroline Diggs was his mom. And she was fearless, all the way to the end.

And she wanted him to do this.

She'd given him more than enough during her life. Time for Curial to start giving back.

He unzipped the backpack and grabbed the sticky slippers and gloves out of his pack and put them on. Then he stuck his foot in a small crevice, took one last breath, and reached his hand up to a stone above.

"It's now or never Curial," said Maurice in Curial's ear.

Curial turned off the transmitter so he could concentrate, made the sign of the cross, and started to climb.

CHAPTER TWENTY-NINE

BREAKING IN

Maurice's Spidey slippers and gloves worked well; they provided incredible stickiness that made climbing up the stone wall easier.

But Curial was only a third of the way up, and already he was shaking, his heart thump-thumping in his chest. His breath never slowed even for a moment, and his hands, though artificially sticky at the moment, were shaking so hard it was as if they wanted to pry him from the wall and throw him to the ground.

Curial stopped climbing, and hugged the stone wall tightly.

And that day flooded back to him.

He was at the top of the ferris wheel, alone. The ride was stuck, and the wind was blowing, and his car kept shaking. His mom was on the ground, waving frantically for him, and all he could do was scream, "Thirty-eight! Thirty-eight! Thirty-eight!"

Through the years since then, his mom had tried to help him get over his fear of heights. She'd even had the climbing wall built in the hopes that slowly, together, they could overcome his fear.

And then she got sick.

And as scared as he'd been on top of that ferris wheel, nothing was scarier than her last few weeks, when he knew she was going to die.

Curial squeezed the rocks with his hands and feet and knees; he buried his head against the stone wall. He couldn't move any farther.

Mom, he thought. *I can't do this.*

And then he heard something. Although it came from inside his own head, he was certain of the voice.

Curial, she said. *Remember how scared you were when you thought I would die? Well guess what? I did die.*

I died and… you're okay. You moved on. You're making me proud. You're on this wall being so brave.

And you know what I want you to do now?

I want you to finish.

She wanted him to finish.

Correction: *he* wanted to finish.

And they could still climb this wall together.

Curial snapped his head up, reached for a rock, and climbed. His heart still beat fast, his body still shook, but on he climbed, one stone at a time, until at last he reached the third-story window and grabbed the sill tightly with both hands. He'd made it. He slid his finger up to his ear and turned the transmitter back on.

"Why the heck did you turn your transmitter off?" barked Maurice.

"So you couldn't talk to me, thereby making me fall, and break every bone in my body," responded Curial.

"I call that mentally weak, Diggs. Whatever. You'll need a Microburst to take care of the Denoyev switch."

"You can tell it's a Denoyev switch from the fence?"

"I'm what you call an optimistic thief," said Maurice.

Curial wedged his slippers into a crevice in the stone and then pressed up against the window sill while he took out a Microburst. He set it carefully on the windowpane.

"Now release the red button and hope that you and I get to sleep in our comfortable American beds the rest of our lives."

"What happened to the optimistic thief?" asked Curial.

"I'm also moody."

Curial released the red button. Three seconds later the window vibrated ever so slightly, and then it was over.

"No presence of an alarm," said Maurice through the earpiece. "I call that a good thing. Now use the knife like I showed you."

Curial slid a knife along the edge of the window, lifted, and—click—the window slid up easily. He pushed it all the way up and peeked his head in. The lights on the third floor were low. No sign of anybody around, though he knew that security guard would be perched at the stairs no more than forty feet away.

Taking a deep breath, Curial lifted himself up and over the window ledge, then dropped as softly as he could onto the floor. He carefully closed the window behind him and advanced on the office door and a very familiar looking device.

"Maurice, I'm telling you this looks exactly like the lock in Koralenko's house."

"Then maybe lady luck is on our side tonight. You'll need to take the electronic bypass and fit it over the keypad."

Just like Maurice instructed, Curial slid the bypass over the keypad. A red wire dangled to the side.

"You see that port on the original keypad?" said Maurice. "It's a small hole just below the numbers and to the right."

Curial scanned until he found it. "Got it."

"Now connect the red wire to the port and let that baby work its magic."

Curial connected the wire to the port and then backed up. The display on the bypass blinked, and then letters started flipping until the display came to a stop.

A – D – E – I – L – N

"You seeing this on your end?" Curial asked.

"Yeah," replied Maurice. "A-D-E-I-L-N. Wait a second. Double check how many number slots are on the original keypad display?"

Curial leaned in. "Five."

"Then this is going to be harder. The bypass gave us six letters."

"What does that mean?"

"These are the six letters used with greatest frequency over the last month. If the display calls for only a five letter code, then that can mean only one thing?"

"And I'm guessing it's not a good thing."

"It means Ardankin changed his password sometime in the last month. That means we have to figure out which four or five of these letters to use. This is where you come in."

"Need I remind you that you're the one sitting behind a computer right now?" said Curial.

"Need I remind you how often you've hinted that you're smarter than me?" said Maurice. "Plus, you *know* Ardankin. You're the best one to figure this out."

Curial looked at the letters again.

A – D – E – I – L – N

One word popped out at him, one word that had something to do with phones. And sometimes in life, the simplest answers were the best. He punched in the code.

D – I – A – L

A red light blinked and a small beep came from the keypad. Then nothing happened.

"Okay, I heard a beep. Was that a good beep?"

"Not exactly. I tried D-I-A-L," said Curial.

"You didn't think about running it past me first?"

Curial slapped himself on the forehead. "Dial" was an English word—but Ardankin would use a *Russian* word. And, as Dina had reminded him repeatedly, Curial was a blockhead who didn't know any Russian. He swallowed hard and took another look at the letters.

A – D – E – I – L – N

Six letters to make a four- or five-digit Russian code. He looked at the last four letters. Wait a second. He may not know any Russian words, but he *did* know some Russian names. Famous Russian names. And one *very* famous Russian name would work.

"How about L-E-N-I-N?" Curial asked.

"That actually seems pretty plausible. I'm okay with it if you are."

Curial took a deep breath and punched in another code.

L – E – N – I – N

The red light blinked, a beep came out and again nothing happened.

"Didn't work."

"Crap," replied Maurice. "It's possible we have two more chances at this. More likely, only one."

"And what happens if we don't get it right?"

"The keypad resets and no one can enter the door for twenty four hours," said Maurice.

And that just wouldn't do. Curial was supposed to be smart enough to do this. He looked at the letters again. He had run out of chances—he had to get it right this time. *Think, Curial. Think.*

"Curial, chances are the key code is going to be special to Ardankin, so he can remember it easily. What is special to Valery Ardankin?

Curial looked at the letters again.

"Maurice, you're a genius."

He typed D-I-N-A into the keypad and pressed enter.

A green light blinked on, three short beeps came out of the keypad and a click came from the door.

"That sounded different, please tell me that sounded different," said Maurice.

"It worked," said Curial.

"Oh thank God."

Curial released a sigh then pushed the door open slowly and stepped into darkness. He slid his hand along the wall, found the switch, and flipped it upward. The lights turned on. And a bedroom, a boy's bedroom came into view.

Along the wall near the switch was a dresser. In the middle of the room was an old bed. At the foot of the bed was a wooden trunk. On the walls were shelves filled with toys. Old toys. And then Curial looked to the far wall. There was a wooden desk and on the wooden desk was a glass case. And inside that glass case....were dolls.

The Romanov Dolls.

Curial stumbled forward. "Maurice, they're here, they're really here!"

Then Curial picked up static in his ear, and a muffled sound of someone...well, shouting.

"Maurice, did you hear me?"

Just then the door behind Curial swung open. He spun around to see Professor Valery Ardankin walk into the room. His hands were in the air and his face was colorless. He was followed by Victor Koralenko. He held a pistol which he turned from the head of Valery Ardankin and now held at the face of Curial.

"Ahhh, young Mr. Diggs, so nice to meet again. You may have heard this before but, I have a gun and I most certainly know how to use it."

CHAPTER THIRTY

BEAUTIFUL DOLLS

"I've made it clear to Professor Ardankin that I can put a bullet through his head faster than he can scream. And I assure you Mr. Diggs, the same is true for you."

Curial was looking from Koralenko to Ardankin.

"Confused?" said Koralenko as he waved the nose of his gun a bit. "I thought so. Oh, and don't even think about your two other friends, Maurice and Miss Ardankin won't be helping you. My men are rounding them up as we speak."

"I don't understand," said Curial.

"I know, I know. It has been so fun to watch you piece it all together. And to think, before you visited me in Moscow I didn't dream there was any chance of ever finding the Romanov Dolls. You see, I've gotten where I've gotten in life by being a man of opportunity. And when you walked into my life, I saw an opportunity. So my men planted a very tiny transmitter on your phone. You'd never notice it, especially when you're being kidnapped at gunpoint riding in a bumpy van." Koralenko smiled. "And since then, I've been tracking you and listening to you. Now granted, I can't hear everything. But I've heard enough, and to watch you solve this mystery has been extraordinary."

"How did you figure it out?" Professor Ardankin asked Curial directly.

Koralenko waved his gun. "Ahh yes, do tell Mr. Diggs, it's all quite fascinating."

Curial clenched his fists. "You can't do this. You *know* who my father is."

"Yes, I do and back in Moscow it wasn't worth the trouble. But now?" Koralenko looked past Curial to the other side of the bed. "Now, I have the Romanov Dolls within my grasp. And the Romanov Dolls are worth whatever mess we create tonight. So please, don't embarrass yourself by trying to scare an old KGB man like myself. Instead, do me the honor and tell us how you figured it all out."

Professor Ardankin looked scared. He knew Koralenko better than Curial did, and there was fear all over his face. That made Curial scared. It was time to play along. And stall. He turned towards Professor Ardankin.

"We figured out the symbol on the bottom of the dolls

was from an old secret police group run by Koralenko's father."

"Which my people on the street heard about, so of course I brought the children in," said Koralenko.

"More like he kidnapped us."

Ardankin's expression changed. "You kidnapped my granddaughter?"

"Now, now, Valery, calm down. Didn't touch a hair on her beautiful head."

Curial continued. "When Koralenko was convinced we weren't spies, he let us go but not before he told us something we'd never heard about the dolls. He said they were created at Abramtsevo."

Koralenko waved the gun again, then tilted his head. "To be honest, Abramtsevo didn't mean much to me. My father said it once, but to a Russian, so many old toys were made at Abramtsevo that it didn't mean anything of significance at all."

"But *I* am not Russian," said Curial, "and had only heard about Abramtsevo in connection with the creation of the first matryoshka dolls, so it felt more like a clue to me. And when we checked the place out, we found a picture: a picture of Vasily Zvyozdochkin, a young apprentice named Ivan Belsky and…well…Rasputin."

Koralenko beamed with pride, as if he had figured it all out himself.

"Extraordinary," said Professor Ardankin.

"We went to the toy museum and figured out that Ivan Belsky was the grandfather of a Gennady Belsky and that he was in fact the same person as Gennady Lukin, the doll maker that you, Professor Ardankin, have known for years. We confronted Gennady and he finally told us the truth, that his grandfather had helped make the Romanov Dolls and that Rasputin took them to give to Czar Nicholas."

Koralenko nodded. "But here Valery, here is where things get exciting."

Curial continued. "Years later, a man came to Abramtsevo by the name of Boris Markov. He befriended Gennady and at some point asked Gennady if he could re-create the Romanov Dolls. So Gennady did his best, and one day Markov picked up the dolls, paid him a handsome sum of money, and left. A week later, the Romanov Dolls were stolen. Two weeks later Boris Markov was dead. Gennady was scared so he and Valeeni packed up and came to St. Petersburg under a new name. But little did they know, they moved to the city of their friend's killer. We found out the murder took place at Koralenko's White Hills estate and thus we assumed Koralenko was behind it all along."

Koralenko smiled. "Until this evening,"

"That's right," said Curial. "Dina was showing me

your house and we came by this room." Curial waved his arm around. "She said it was always locked and nobody ever went in. Nobody but you. I asked her why. Dina said it was her Uncle Nikolai's room who died when he was quite young. Had a terrible disease. Hemophilia. Coincidentally enough, it was same disease Alexei Romanov had."

Curial noticed Professor Ardankin's face shift a little.

"And that's when everything started to come together. Rasputin was a sorcerer, a healer and many people have always thought he did something to help heal Alexei of his hemophilia. And what I figured was Rasputin did something to those dolls, something that none of us can understand, and those dolls helped heal Alexei."

If possible, even more color drained from Ardankin's face.

"And further, Professor Ardankin, I guessed that you somehow discovered this too. And you figured the dolls just might be able to save your only son."

Koralenko beamed like a proud parent. "Brilliant don't you think Valery? And to think you used your position at my father's estate to pull off an enormous art heist and then, instead of sharing the treasure with the Koralenkos, you kept it for yourself. And you killed the thief so nobody would ever know. Amazing."

"What's even more amazing is the cowardly way in

which Valery took Markov out. Shot him right in the back. He said Markov was a thief, that's what he told father and I. Valery said he was just protecting our estate. So, naturally, father and I stood up for him, protected him from the police. And to think, all along you killed Markov for your personal gain. You greedy, greedy man."

Ardankin shook his head. "No Victor, you don't understand."

Victor cocked back on the revolver. "No Valery, I think I do."

And that's when it hit Curial. Koralenko doesn't *know*. He hadn't quite figured it all out. And that meant Curial just might have a chance.

Curial took a small step towards Koralenko. "So what are you going to do, just kill us and take the Romanov Dolls for yourself?"

Koralenko made a face. "The thought had crossed my mind. A suspicious American breaks into a respected Russian's house and then he and the respected Russian die in a hail of bullets. Of course, since I am KGB, I will make sure the police draw those conclusions. I believe I told you I haven't killed anybody in a while and frankly, it's making me a bit itchy."

Curial should have been scared. He should have been shaking. But he wasn't. Koralenko was a bully, and Curial's entire family legacy was built on standing up to bullies. He took another small step. "So, just like that. *My* mother searched for these dolls her whole life, *I* did all the work, and then *you're* going to swoop in at the last moment and take them away."

Koralenko shrugged, amusement all over his face. "As opposed to?"

Curial held out his hands, palms out. "At least let me look at them, touch them, My God, are you such a monster that you can't at least give me that?"

Koralenko waved his gun back and forth and danced his tongue along his lip. Finally he threw one of his hands in the air. "Oh, I must be getting old and soft. Fine. Dying wish, blah, blah, blah. Touch the dolls, lick them. Just don't do anything stupid."

Koralenko went for it. And unfortunately at this point, doing something stupid was Curial's only chance at getting out of this mess. He turned from Koralenko and passed by Professor Ardankin. As he did, Professor Ardankin seemed to look right through him. Curial walked around the bed to the other side of the room. He went to the desk, where the glass case was. Where the Romanov Dolls were.

"Easy now," Koralenko said from behind.

Curial looked at them, really looked at them. He had seen pictures, he had heard his mother talk about them. He had dreamed of this moment, of finally coming face to face with this brilliant treasure. These dolls were indeed beautiful.

But as he looked at them now, he knew with certainty what he had only guessed before. They weren't perfect.

Curial carefully lifted the case up and wrapped both hands over the largest of the dolls. Heavier than it looked. It should do the trick just fine.

But he had to be certain.

He gently turned the largest doll so he could see the bottom. Just as he'd guessed.

No symbol.

He saw Ardankin give him a funny look and then Curial squared up on Koralenko and raised his arms. He took a step and, as he jumped up to the bed, he threw the doll as hard as he could right at Koralenko's head. As Curial hit the bed he jumped again, this time directly towards Koralenko.

Koralenko fired his gun wildly into the air as the doll connected with the old Russian's chin. Curial hit the ground and charged him and, as Koralenko fumbled for the revolver, Curial blasted him with an overhand right that smashed into Koralenko's nose. Koralenko fell back and screamed in pain just as the door flew open and a large Russian man came in holding a gun, he fired it once into the room and Professor Ardankin screamed as he jumped in front of Curial. Meanwhile, Curial rolled to the side then kicked the large man in the side of the knee. As the man cried out in pain, Curial grabbed the doll and smashed it into the side of the large man's head. The man's eyes instantly started to circle the drain, and then he dropped his weapon and fell into a motionless heap right on top of Victor Koralenko.

Curial ran over to Ardankin and put his hand on top of Professor Ardankin's right shoulder, pressing down.

"I've never been shot before," the Professor said.

"You saved my life," said Curial.

"I'm not a good man Curial. I killed a man."

Curial looked back. The large man was motionless and Koralenko couldn't move. He turned back. "But it wasn't like Koralenko said, was it Professor Ardankin? You didn't murder Markov and I don't think you killed him to shut him up."

Ardankin moved his head back and forth slowly. "I've replayed that day in my head for the last forty-four years. Markov brought me the Romanov Dolls and I thought my son Nikolai was saved. My boy was dying and I would have done anything for him. And then after a few minutes, I could tell. The dolls, they were beautiful but...well...*you* could see it...I saw the look in your eyes."

"But the dolls weren't perfect," said Curial.

Ardankin nodded. "I demanded to know what Markov

did with the real dolls. He said I was crazy. But I knew he was lying. I pulled out a revolver to scare him, only to scare him and he ran away."

"And that's when you fired?"

Now Ardankin's eyes were wet. "I thought if I shot close to him that he would know I was serious. That he would tell me the truth. But…oh dear God, I hit him. I hit him square in the back. He died in my arms within minutes."

Just then a chill ran down Curial's spine. "Maurice, and Dina! Koralenko said his men had gathered them up."

"My phone," Ardankin gasped. "Check my phone. Ever since you came to St. Petersburg, I've had someone following my Dina."

"A large man in a dark trench coat?" Curial asked.

Ardankin nodded.

Curial fished the phone out of Ardankin's pocket then held it in front of him. He pushed a button and the phone started ringing. A man answered after one ring.

"Status report," Ardankin managed to say.

"Had some trouble with Victor Koralenko's men but everything is fine now."

"So Dina is safe?"

"Not only Dina but the little annoying one as well," said the voice.

"Maurice?" Curial said. Ardankin nodded.

The man on the phone continued. "Dina was already headed back to the house when Koralenko's men tried to grab her. Then we found Maurice surrounded by goons when we got back."

"So where are you now?" asked Ardankin.

"I made the annoying one wait at the front gate but I'm bringing Dina into the house as we speak."

Ardankin froze and grabbed Curial by the shirt. "My granddaughter, she can't know. She can't know what I've done."

"What do you expect me to tell her?"

"Curial Diggs, you must do this for me. If she knew the truth about me, that I'm a killer, it would destroy her. Plus, Koralenko is right. He *is* KGB. I can handle him but things are bound to get very messy once people know Americans are involved. You need to leave the country and you need to leave now!"

"Fine, but first I say goodbye to Dina," said Curial. Ardankin shook his head.

"Do you like my granddaughter?"

"Well yes."

"Then please, please don't do this to her."

The door flew open, Dina looked down and ran to her grandfather. She saw the blood and her eyes grew huge. She saw Curial and her face became confused. "W-what happened?"

Dina looked at her grandfather and then at Curial again. She knelt down beside them. It was Ardankin who spoke first.

"Curial must leave before Koralenko's people get here."

"What?" she said, clearly confused.

Curial stood up and swallowed.

"Curial, what did you do to my grandfather!? What's going on?"

"Go Curial now!" Ardankin managed to get out.

And all Curial could do was nod his head helplessly. "I'm so sorry Dina." Then he turned around and jogged out the door.

CHAPTER THIRTY-ONE

UNLIMITED HOT DOGS

Robert Mercury Diggs didn't even see his son when Curial got back into town the next day. Instead, Curial received a text from Getty, saying the President of Diggs Banks was preparing for another trip and wouldn't see his only son until the middle of the following week.

And Getty reminded him of his test in two days.

Good old dad. Good old Getty.

Curial lay face down on his bed, counting the fibers in his carpet. Ever since he, Maurice, and Mike had boarded the plane to come home from Russia, Curial had been depressed. His mother had given him a task—in some ways, it was her whole life's work—and he had been *so close*... only to find that even those closest to the truth had no idea what had happened to the *real* Romanov dolls.

And if his dad ever found out what had happened in

Russia, Curial would be on the next train to Haverfield, right after his dad reminded him that the life he and the rest of the Diggs men had carved out for Curial wasn't so bad.

Maybe it was time to start remembering that.

Curial's door burst open. Maurice stood there, looking at his phone and smiling.

"I've got an important art gallery party to attend tonight and it looks like my date hasn't even showered," said Maurice.

"I'm not really in the mood," said Curial.

"I'm not sure it matters if you're 'in the mood.' You told me yourself, your friend Claude needs you. Plus... what would your mother do?"

Curial breathed in through his nostrils and sat up. "I really hope you don't pull the what-would-my-mother do line on me often."

Maurice scratched his chin. "I'm not sure. I wonder what your mother would do?"

"Isn't there a small country you could annoy right now?"

"Ahh Curial, I'm not here to annoy you. We'll have plenty of time for that later. Nope, I'm here about the Romanov Dolls."

"Don't remind me."

"Hear me out," said Maurice. "I think there's still a

chance to find them. I'm not sure you've looked at every possibility."

"Forget it, we went through all of this on the plane."

Maurice smiled. "Are you sure? He handed Curial a yellow folder and he opened it up.

Curial examined the contents. "These are the employee files and interviews from the time of the theft. Come on, we've already been over these dozens of times. There's nothing here. And on the plane ride home…"

"I know: we went through every employee again to see if anybody was related to Markoff."

"And nothing," said Curial firmly.

"Nothing, my dear boy"—Maurice pointed at him—"because you think like a boy."

"I *am* a boy. So are you."

"But I'm a mature boy. More of a man really. Evolved is what people tell me."

Curial threw a pillow and hit Maurice in the head. "And anyways," Maurice continued, "Mr. Impatient Rich Kid, it is a proven fact that less evolved boys routinely overlook fifty percent of the population."

"Meaning what?" said Curial.

"Don't send a boy to do a job only a woman can do."

"So now you're a woman?" asked Curial.

"Not me," said Maurice.

"Then who?"

"Like I said, don't send a boy to do a job only a woman can do."

With that, Maurice stepped to the side and smiled. And someone appeared at the door. Someone Curial never expected to see again. She was his age, blonde, and was dressed in a red party dress. Curial shot off the bed.

"Dina?" He said.

Her expression was half excited to see him and half she wanted to punch his lights out.

"To think you could walk away like that with just *I'm really sorry?*"

"But I, I didn't know what to do."

She rolled her eyes then looked at Maurice. "Blockhead." Then Dina smiled. "But I forgive you...and...well, grandfather told me everything."

"He told you *everything* everything?"

"Unlike you, I'm not an idiot. When you and Maurice failed to show up at Koralenko's house, I knew something was wrong. And in case you didn't notice, my grandfather had a bullet in him and you left in that totally weird way. First thing my grandfather did was have Koralenko arrested. Second thing he did was go to the hospital. I was with him all night and he finally broke down and told me the truth. It's not every day you learn your grandfather is a killer."

"I don't think it's quite as simple as that," said Curial.

"I don't either," said Dina. "Anyways, he eventually went to sleep and I had a lot of time alone in the hospital room to think things over. And of course, if Grandfather really had the fake dolls all those years, then the question is—"

"*Where* are the real Romanov Dolls?" said Curial. "I know, it's all I can think about."

"And while you were feeling sorry for yourself on this bed, I was doing something about it. I wondered to myself if Boris Markov had any family. Turns out he had a sister. And do you know where this sister moved to? America. Specifically, New York. Her name? Irene Markov."

Dina smiled and she and Maurice exchanged a look like they knew a secret.

"Out with it you two," said Curial.

Maurice folded his arms. "And do you know what makes Irene Markov special?"

"I'm sure hoping you both will tell me."

"Turns out," Dina began, "that Irene worked at the MAC when the Romanov Dolls were stolen."

"What?" said Curial.

"You heard her Curial," said Maurice. "After Dina gave me the information, I did the search myself and sure enough, Irene Markov definitely worked at the MAC."

"But that's not possible, I've been over the employee lists dozens of times, there's no Irene Markov."

Dina shook her head and sighed. "Boys. Boys *always* forget that women are routinely forced to change their names."

"Oh no. Not again," Curial said while thinking back to Gennady and Valeeni.

"Oh yes," said Dina.

Maurice grabbed the folder and flipped through to a picture of a woman with dark brown hair, in her early thirties.

Curial scanned her name and looked up. "Irene Johnson. Wait, we already looked at her. Her name's on that exhibit in the MAC, the one that honors deceased members of the MAC family. She's the woman who was hit by the bus the day after the heist. Tragic, I'll give you that. But we looked into it. The death was an accident. Nothing suspicious about it at all."

"True," said Maurice. "But listen to this: Irene married Gill Johnson in 1965. Before that, her name, verified by the state of New York, was Irene Markoff."

Curial looked at Maurice, a wide smile spreading across his face. "How did you figure it out?"

"I've spent an exhausting morning with a very large and hairy woman down at the city records office, and she helped me go through every single female employee, just in case."

"You did?"

Maurice stood on his toes. "Don't worry Diggs, my shoulders are big enough to carry you. Anyways, Irene and her husband are long gone, but her daughter Maria lives in Brooklyn. I called and she's expecting you."

"Me?"

"No Curial, she's expecting the both of you." Maurice wagged his finger at Dina and then Curial. "Frankly, I'm exhausted from doing all the work around here. Plus, I need to go steal money from a bunch of rich people who don't know how to play Three Card Monte. Figured you two lovebirds could handle it from here."

"But Curial," Dina said as she wrinkled her nose. "You kinda stink. So first, take a shower, put on your tux, and then meet me outside."

*_*_*

Thirty minutes later, Mike dropped Curial and Dina off in front of a small home in south Brooklyn.

They walked up the steps and rang the bell. A blond woman in her early fifties answered the door. She looked at Dina, then at Curial, and finally put her hands on her hips. "Did I miss my invite for the prom?"

Dina smiled. "Thank you so much, Maria, for seeing us on such short notice."

Maria stared at Curial the way he'd been stared at his whole life. "You're that Diggs kid, aren't you?"

Curial smiled and extended his hand and she laughed.

"Well, a famous kid and a girl as pretty as you? Not every day I have royalty in my home. Come in. I was wondering if anybody was ever going to talk to me about this."

"About what?" asked Curial.

The woman led them into her living room and sat down on a comfortable chair. She motioned for them to take the couch. "I may live in a small place in Brooklyn, but I'm no idiot. The Romanov Dolls were stolen when I was nine years old, and all these years I've wondered if somebody would find them."

Curial leaned forward. "Your mom, she died the day after the theft?"

The woman laid her hands in her lap. "We didn't know about the theft of course. She was on her way to work, bus hit her. Mom didn't have a chance."

"I'm very sorry. I—I know what it's like to lose your mom."

Maria shook her head gently. "It's okay. It was a long time ago." She smiled. "It gets easier, I promise."

Curial didn't know what to say.

Maria broke the awkward silence. "So, what did you want to know?"

Dina leaned forward. "Your mom's maiden name, Markoff. That's Russian."

"Yeah, she found her way to America, met my dad. She left a brother back in Russia, named Boris. I never knew him. Coincidentally, he died same year she did."

Curial and Dina exchanged a look. Curial jumped in. "Do you know anything, anything at all, about what happened to the Romanov Dolls?"

Maria shrugged. "No, but I think my mom knew something about it."

"Why do you say that?" asked Dina.

"The week before she died, something was wrong. Mom was stressed out, pacing around our home, hadn't done her hair in days—and my mother *always* did her hair. So the night before she died, she was rewashing a set of pots and pans for probably the third time when I finally asked her what was wrong. She turned to me and I saw that she had been crying.

"She bent down and ruffled my hair, she told me she loved me... that's why I'll never forget this—it was the last time she told me she loved me. She told me she had done something bad and that she had to fix it, or something much worse would happen.

"I didn't know what any of that meant, but it made me scared. And then, two days later, on the way to work, she was hit by a bus and killed instantly. I think that maybe she was so worried about whatever was going on, she wasn't paying attention, wasn't looking where she was going."

Dina sat up straight. "Maria, what exactly do you think your mother was talking about?"

"I can't be sure of course. And at the time... Well, I was nine, my mother had just died, and she was my whole world—I didn't think about it. But as the years went on and the Romanov Dolls stayed missing, I thought about them more. And I'm convinced that they were what mother was talking about."

Curial checked his watch. "Thank you, Maria, for sharing your story."

"You think it will help find the dolls?"

He smiled. "I hope."

They left Miss Johnson's place and climbed into the back of Mike's car. Dina looked at Curial. "Well, what do you think?"

"Let's work it through. Irene Markoff Johnson is helping her brother Boris steal the Romanov Dolls, except at the last minute she's having second thoughts. She apparently can't convince her brother not to do it, and she doesn't want him to get caught. So that night after work, and before Boris comes into the museum..."

"She steals the dolls herself?" Dina suggested.

Curial frowned.

Dina leaned in. "That would explain why she was so jumpy the next day going to work, why she was so distracted."

Curial was shaking his head. "But it doesn't fit. She steals them and then… what? She's just going to put them back? Why take the risk of taking them outside of the museum when…" Curial's eyes popped and he snapped his fingers.

"What?" said Dina.

Curial took a deep breath as his shoulders shot up. "She wouldn't. She wouldn't take them outside of the museum. Could it really be that simple?"

He sat up, his eyes wide. "Mike! Hot dogs for a month if you can get us to the MAC in ten minutes."

"Ten minutes in this traffic? Can't be done, sir."

"*Unlimited* hot dogs," said Curial.

"And my wife won't hear about this?"

"Not a chance."

"Buckle your seatbelts," said Mike.

CHAPTER THIRTY-TWO

PERFECT

While Curial sent a series of texts to Maurice, Mike violated just about every traffic law in New York City—and a few laws of physics—and nine minutes later, Curial and Dina were running up the steps of the MAC. The crowd was streaming in, a good crowd to be sure, but not the crowd that would have been there to see the Egyptian Queen Sefronia's jewels.

Curial and Dina squeezed through the crowd and Curial spotted Claude across the way, greeting guests. He was smiling, like the pro that he was, but even from across the room, Curial could tell: Claude was putting on a brave face.

He might not have to act brave for long.

Curial ran toward him, the crowd reacting loudly to a thirteen-year-old black kid in a tuxedo running through such a dignified setting.

The always-refined Claude looked horrified. "Mr.

Diggs? What on earth?"

Curial was out of breath, more from excitement than from the short sprint. "Claude, you need to come with me right now."

"Mr. Diggs, I'm sorry but I'm in the middle—"

Curial grabbed his forearm. "Right now!" Curial pulled and Claude gave in, and together they jogged to the newly opened exhibition hall.

"Curial," Claude whispered, "what is the meaning of this?"

Curial stopped in front of the photo gallery that showed the MAC through the ages.

"My mom told me, more than once, that if only these walls could talk, maybe they'd be able to tell us about what really happened to the Romanov Dolls."

Claude looked around, clearly embarrassed, as a crowd formed around them. He leaned in, gritting his teeth. "I know what your mom used to say," he muttered, "but tonight is *not* the night."

"I think tonight is the *perfect* night. And maybe, just maybe, these walls *can* talk." Curial stepped forward to a set of pictures. "Claude, you told me that when the dolls were stolen, the MAC was in the middle of its first renovation. You said this picture of the east part of the exhibition wall shows the wall as it existed then. Isn't that correct?"

"Yes, but—"

"From the file, I read that it was the construction crew who first discovered that the dolls were missing."

Claude looked around nervously. "Yes, the next morning. They got to work early and then they noticed the missing dolls. But what does this have to do with anything?"

Curial scanned the crowd quickly, and then, spotting someone, hollered out. "Brian!"

A man wearing a brown sports coat and jeans pointed to himself. It was Brian, the man who had been foreman of the construction crew for this latest renovation. Brian walked nervously over.

Claude stepped closer and mumbled under his breath. "Curial, you're making an incredible scene. What is going on?"

Curial ignored him and took Brian by the arm. "Brian, you see this photo of the east wall of the exhibition hall back in 1970? Can you show me exactly where that is?"

Brian leaned in, took a look at the photo, then popped back up. "Sure." He walked toward the wall, with Curial and Dina following. In fact, the entire group was following now, not understanding what was going on, but entranced by the scene. "Right here. Instead of covering up everything to make it look new, we've kept the old lines so you can see the evolution of the museum through the years."

Curial looked around. Dina nodded at him and smiled. Claude and the board members of the museum had formed a tight circle around him and it seemed the entire party had now crowded into the exhibition hall to see what was going on.

"Curial, please," said Claude through gritted teeth. "I don't know what has come over you, but this, this has to stop."

"No Claude, we need to tell the truth of what happened so many years ago." Curial cleared his throat and addressed the gathering crowd.

"As most of you know, my mother loved the Manhattan Art Collective, and she loved the people who gave their lives to it, like Claude Von Kerstens. And, from the time she first saw them when she was a little girl, she loved the Romanov Dolls. She told me about them when I was little; the mystery behind them became the great bedtime story of my youth. My mother died this past year, but she wanted me to keep looking for and thinking about those beautiful dolls."

Right then, Curial spotted an extremely short Jewish Rabbi walking towards him dragging a ten-pound sledge hammer across the floor. He bumped through a few people and then heaved the sledge over to Curial.

"Thank you Rabbi…"

"Shullman, Rabbi Shullman. One of my best disguises,

now defiled since I had to come out of character to obtain this impossibly large hammer. Oy vey, my back is killing me," said Maurice.

A horrified expression crossed Claude's face. "And what are you proposing to do with that?"

Curial kept the sledge behind him and raised his finger into the air. "But what if the dolls were never stolen? What if they were *going* to be stolen, and then somebody—in order to protect the dolls—decided to *hide* them instead?"

One of the board members stepped forward. It was Chairman Nelson. "What are you talking about?"

"I'm talking about this." Curial picked up the sledge hammer and, with everything he had, let it fly directly into the wall. There was a loud, thunderous *smash* as the hammer exploded through the wall. Claude, Nelson, and the rest of the board members covered their faces, but when Curial picked up the sledge again, a couple of the board members rushed forward to stop him.

Dina and Maurice stepped in their way.

"Listen, boys," said Dina. "No family has given more money and more time and more passion to this museum than the Diggs family."

One of the board members tried to say something, but Maurice barked something in Yiddish while stomping his boot to the ground.

"Let's see what this is all about, okay?" said Dina.

Curial continued to let loose on the wall, and after a couple of minutes he had opened up a two-foot by four-foot hole, right where the wall would have extended back in 1970. He finally put down the sledge hammer, looked at Maurice, smiled at Dina and took a deep breath.

Dina put a hand on his shoulder and squeezed.

Curial climbed into the hole in the wall, getting plaster dust all over his tuxedo, and started looking sideways down the inside of the wall. He pushed his face in deeper; he should have brought a flashlight.

"The boy has gone insane, Claude," Nelson said. "This is beyond embarrassing."

Claude snapped back. "For once, Mr. Nelson, step back and shut your mouth."

Curial was staring into darkness, stretching with his arm, coming up against wood studs, wires, metal and cobwebs, and plaster dust.

And then he hit something. It was smooth and soft like cloth. Like a small pillowcase. His heart raced. He stretched and grabbed hold of it. He grabbed and pulled, and when he got it out of the wall cavity, he held it against his belly. Inside the cloth was something small, hard, and dense.

He turned around and climbed out of the hole in the wall. He looked at Dina, then at Claude. He smiled, and handed the bag to Claude.

"I think someone wanted to make sure these were never, ever stolen," said Curial. "Go ahead."

Claude accepted the cloth bag like it was the baby Jesus, and slowly—a lump clearly forming in his throat—began to untie the bag. Curial peered inside as Claude opened the bag. The object inside was gold, shiny, and lined with jewels.

A beautiful matryoshka doll. And it had been hidden away for over forty years, undisturbed, just waiting to be found.

"Oh my God," Claude said, tears in his eyes as he pulled the Romanov Dolls out and started to un-nest them, turning so the crowd could see.

The crowd reacted with amazement, oohing and ahhing. The entire exhibition hall was suddenly filled with a hubbub of excitement.

Curial felt a hand slide down his arm and interlace its fingers with his and then squeeze. He turned to look at Dina, her eyes were wet with tears.

She sounded like she'd lost her breath. "Curial, they're…."

"Perfect," he said.

CHAPTER THIRTY-THREE

WELL DONE

At the insistence of the thirteen-year-old kid with the famous last name who had discovered the Romanov Dolls, the board decided to keep Claude Von Kerstens on in his position as the Director of the Manhattan Art Collective. And the next month was quite busy for Claude as he planned another grand reopening for the MAC, this time inviting the entire art world to see their glorious rediscovered treasure.

Claude was also busy with some delicate negotiations with the Russian art community, negotiations that resulted in a compromise which pleased his young treasure-hunting friend. For four months each year, the Romanov Dolls would be held at Winter Palace Museum in St. Petersburg—and in exchange, during this time, an assortment of Russian art would be featured at the MAC.

Claude also had to find an artist to put together an extremely important piece very quickly.

The night of the grand opening was incredible. Curial had never seen so many people, and much of the night was embarrassing to him. It was hard to have all those people looking at him. He didn't find the Romanov Dolls to gain their accolades; he did it for much more personal reasons. So when all the talking was done and the schmoozing began, Curial escaped from the crowd and found a quiet empty corner of the museum, where he sat on a bench in front of a painting of a beautiful woman. A new painting.

He heard footsteps behind him and turned to see Claude sitting down next to him.

"You did a great job," Curial said, nodding at the painting. "It looks just like her."

Claude smiled. "I told the artist I needed the finest painting in the world for the finest woman I've ever known. And I told him he had only two weeks to paint it."

"She'd be embarrassed by it," said Curial.

Claude nodded, then pointed his index finger at the painting. "Yes, but I think she'd like that little trace of a smile."

"Kind of like she knew something the rest of us didn't."

"Exactly. Well, duty calls. Thank you again, Curial, for everything. I can't possibly—"

"You're welcome, Claude."

Curial sat there, quietly looking at the painting of his mother. He had done all this for her. And, incredibly, his dad was none the wiser. Two days after he found the dolls in the wall of the MAC, he took Getty's impossible test. He hoped he did well enough to avoid Haverfield, but he had no idea.

But right now, he didn't much care. He had done it. He had fulfilled his mom's last wish and no matter what happened with Getty or with Haverfield, Curial knew for certain that he would find a way to follow his true ambition in life.

To be a treasure hunter.

Curial saw Mike Douglas walking toward him with his wife. The two of them looked incredible together. And somehow, Mike looked skinny.

"Doesn't my husband look fabulous?" Mrs. Douglas said as she patted her husband's belly. "Mike hasn't been able to button this jacket in five years. I'm so proud of him. Well, Curial, enjoy the evening." Mrs. Douglas walked off and Mike bent down.

"I didn't actually lose any weight," Mike whispered.

"Didn't think you would, on the unlimited hot dog diet," said Curial.

"I've wrapped my belly with four rolls of duct tape."

"And she has no idea?"

"She thinks I got on a fitness kick when I was in Russia."

"And how much pain are you in right now?"

Mike grimaced. "After I take my wife home I'll be checking myself into the hospital."

"You're a strange man, Mike Douglas."

Mike smiled and winced at the same time. "Anything for love, Curial. Anything for love."

Mike left to follow his wife, and Curial had just returned his attention to the painting when he heard footsteps behind him, and figured Mike was back to say something else. But when he turned, standing behind him was a tall black man wearing a grey suit and holding a long white walking stick.

"Matthew!" Curial said as he stood up. "You made it."

"I wouldn't miss it. What are you doing over here all alone?"

Matthew maneuvered around the bench and then sat down next to Curial.

"I'm looking at a painting of my mother that Claude recently had commissioned."

"Ahhhh." Matthew stared at the painting then smiled a big toothy grin. "It's beautiful."

"How can you tell?"

"Because your mom was beautiful."

"And how could you know that? You're blind."

"But I'm also a man. And a man knows when he's in the presence of a beautiful lady. What's the painting called?"

"I told Claude to leave it untitled," said Curial, "but I know what I call it. *Portrait of a Woman Who Knew Almost Everything.*"

Matthew laughed. "I like that very much."

The two continued to look at the painting—a thirteen-year-old treasure hunter and a seventy-year-old blind ex-thief. After a couple minutes, Matthew got up.

"Curial, I still can't believe all the clues you tracked down. Your mother told me you were smart, but I think it's more than that. It takes more than smarts to schedule a meeting with the very man who was behind the whole thing. Nope, Curial, I think you've got a gift for this kind of thing."

"Matthew, I gotta be honest. Maurice did a ton to help and he deserves as much credit as me."

Matthew made a face. "Maybe. By the way, where is my nephew? I thought he'd be appearing tonight."

Curial looked over his shoulder at the short bearded security guard in the corner. "He's been pretending to be a security guard tonight."

"Well, I'll be," said Matthew thoughtfully. "Usually I can smell his sneaky stench a mile away."

Curial laughed. "I think he might have used an entire bottle of Axe body spray to mask his usual smell."

Matthew made a face. "Did you say body spray?"

"Sure, why?"

Matthew started fidgeting for his pockets. Finally, he shook his head. "Well I'll be. That little stinker."

The short bearded security guard was moving towards them now, a brown leather wallet in his hand. "That's right Matthew, I got you. I got you and you didn't even see, hear, or smell me coming."

Curial laughed. "Don't tell me, did he get you with the Old Ruby?"

Matthew frowned. "Worse, he got me with a young Ruby. Some young lady bumped into me, and all I could smell was her perfume along with the overpowering scent of male body spray. I didn't think anything of it."

"Admit it Uncle Matthew," said Maurice, "I'm the best."

"Well, I guess every dog has his day," said Matthew.

"Was that a compliment?" asked Maurice.

Matthew rolled his eyes. "It's the closest you're gonna get from me."

"Then I'll take it."

Matthew laughed. "You know, Curial—back before all this started, I believe you said you'd been looking into a treasure down in Peru?"

"Yeah," said Curial, "what about it?"

"I may have found some information that could be helpful."

"Really? What is it?"

Matthew laughed. "Not tonight. You and Maurice come by my office in the park, let an old man school you at chess, and then we'll talk. Tonight is a celebration— and you need to get back in there and have some fun."

"No offense, but hanging out with a bunch of old people is not my idea of fun."

Matthew laughed. "Too bad. That young lady I ran into while Maurice pulled the young Ruby? Just so happened she said she was looking for you. And she was beautiful."

"How could you know she was beautiful?" asked Curial.

Matthew tapped his walking stick against the tile. "A man always knows. Plus, her English was layered with a Russian accent."

Curial popped up. *She said she couldn't make it.* "Did you say Russian?"

Matthew laughed. "She may have even offered her name. Now what was that?"

Curial got up and sprinted away. "Her name is Dina!" he yelled as he ran past.

"That's one heckuva guess," said Matthew with a laugh. "Like I said kid, you've got a gift."

When Curial found Dina wandering the hallway, he just about lost his breath. She wore a long white dress, had on gold earrings, and her hair fell in a long braid. Matthew was right. She *was* beautiful.

When she saw Curial, at first she smiled. Then she stuck one hand against her hip and glared at him.

"You didn't really think I would miss this did you?" she said.

"Well, when you said 'I'm going to miss this' I thought that might be a clue."

She laughed. "What can I say, my mom wanted to visit New York."

Curial noticed a woman who looked like a larger version of Dina hovering about twenty feet away. Dina saw him looking.

"Yes, that's my mother. Speaking of the truth, I figured that if Grandfather could tell me what he had done, I could come clean with my mother."

"About ballet?" said Curial.

Dina nodded. "I told her. She wasn't happy, but compared to learning her father killed a man, it actually went over pretty well. She decided the two of us need to spend more time together. We agreed that a trip to New York might do us some good." Dina smiled and raised up on her tiptoes. "I'm going to the ballet tonight and need an escort." She held up three tickets.

"Oh," Curial said, pointing his thumb at his chest. "You mean *me*? At the ballet? With you and your *mom*?"

Dina grabbed Curial by the hand and dragged him

toward her mother. Curial's throat went dry. "But I've never been to the ballet before," he said.

Dina smiled. "You'd also never been to Russia before, and look how that turned out."

She was right, of course. Dina Ardankin was beautiful and brilliant, just like another woman Curial had known. He turned and took one last look into the quiet gallery where the MAC's newest painting hung. He gazed at the beautiful woman with the tiny smile. He smiled back.

I love you, Mom.

Dina spun around. "And we're not going to the ballet with my mother. She hates ballet. I figured Maurice would want to come with us. I assume he's around here somewhere."

The short security guard rolled up alongside them. "Hey Dina."

Dina looked, then laughed. "I think I preferred you when you were blind. Well, are you boys ready?" She charged ahead but Maurice tugged on Curial's tuxedo coat.

"Come on Dude, you gotta tell me how you keep recognizing me in my disguises."

Curial rolled his eyes.

"Come on man," said Maurice, "you promised."

Curial stopped. "Fine, I'll explain. But once, and only once, so pay attention."

"Got it."

"The way I keep recognizing you? Well I guess…" Curial hesitated.

"Just spill it okay, I've got street cred riding on this."

"Well I guess a guy just knows when his best friend is around," said Curial.

Maurice's mouth fell open. "Did you just say?"

"Best friend? Yeah, and it's the last time I'll say it."

"I think I feel a hug coming on."

"No you don't," said Curial, "that's just gas. Now come on, we can't be late to our first ballet."

Curial and Maurice followed Dina out of the museum, down the steps, and then took a right. That's when Curial noticed the long black Lincoln pull up. Not the Lincoln Mike usually drove.

This was his father's car.

The door opened, and the always distinguished figure of Robert Mercury Diggs stepped out. Curial froze.

"Father?"

"Hi Curial."

"But I thought you had a trip?"

"I'm headed to the airport now."

His father shifted from side to side. Something was wrong.

"Getty went over the scores from your most recent test."

Curial tensed up.

"They weren't great," said Mr. Diggs.

"But I can—"

"But they weren't terrible either," his father continued. "I told Getty that you're smart, you're a hard worker, and you'll do better in the future."

Curial exchanged looks with Maurice and Dina and then turned back to his father.

"Yes, sir, I will. You can count on that."

Mr. Diggs shifted in his stance. "And there was something else."

Curial felt the hairs stand up on the back of his neck. "Something else?" he replied.

"I talked with Hank earlier today."

Oh no.

"Father, I can explain."

"He told me that you had something to do with finding The Romanov Dolls in the walls of the museum."

"He told you that?" Curial said.

Mr. Diggs nodded. "Pretty clever how you pieced all of that together from nothing more than a comment your mother made and a hunch."

Curial held his breath.

"Well, whatever it was, I just wanted to say, I know…well, I know your mother is very proud of you."

"She is?"

Robert Diggs nodded. Then he walked back to the Lincoln and opened up the door. But before getting back in, he turned back around. "And Curial?"

"Yes sir?"

"Well done."

Curial's throat tightened as he looked at his father. His father returned the look then began to climb back into the car. Finally, Curial managed to say something.

"Thanks, Dad."

Robert Diggs hesitated, his hand on the door, then smiled just a little and climbed back in. The car pulled away and into the late night New York traffic towards the airport and whatever city his father had business in next. Then Curial Diggs took a deep breath, laughed, and followed a Russian and a pickpocket to the ballet.

THE END

CHECK OUT THESE OTHER AWESOME BOOKS BY DANIEL KENNEY!

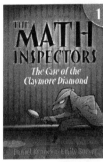
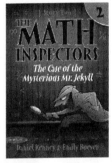
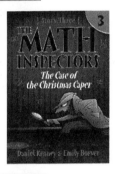

Visit my Amazon Author page at
www.amazon.com/Daniel-Kenney/e/B00NMVQ1ES
for more information

ABOUT THE AUTHOR—DANIEL KENNEY

Daniel Kenney and his wife Teresa live in Omaha, Nebraska with zero cats, zero dogs, one gecko, and lots of kids. When those kids aren't driving him nuts, Daniel is busy writing books, cheering on the Benedictine Ravens, and plotting to take over the world. He is the author of other great books for young readers including The Beef Jerky Gang, The Math Inspectors series, and The Big Life of Remi Muldoon series. Find more information at www.DanielKenney.com.

65990148R00172

Made in the USA
Middletown, DE
06 March 2018